SOUL CRUSHING

St. Leasing – Book Five

L.P. Maxa

ALSO BY L.P. MAXA

RiffRaff Records

Royalty

Legacy

Infamy

Loyalty

Sanctuary

Piracy

Certainty

The Devil's Share

Play Nice

Play Dirty

Play Fair

Play Softly

Play Hard

Play For Keeps

St. Leasing

Mouth Watering

Breath Taking

Jaw Dropping

Heart Stopping

Other Novels

Happy Place

Stumbled into Love

Rescued

www.BOROUGHSPUBLISHINGGROUP.com

SOUL CRUSHING
Copyright © 2019 L.P. Maxa

ISBN 978-1-951055-06- 6

To everyone who loved these shifters enough to want more.
Thank you.

ACKNOWLEDGMENTS

As always, thank you to my wonderful husband and my brilliant daughter. I procrastinate and then bury myself into the creative process, and you guys never make me feel bad about it. Thanks to my mom who helped me flush out this story when I was stuck. To my editor for her never ending patience. To my Smitten Kittens for inspiring me, and for reading my books–all of your messages and comments, they mean the absolute world to me.

SOUL CRUSHING

"I guess to them it's a terrifying thought,
a red riding hood who knew exactly what she was doing when she
invited the wild in."
–Nikita Gill

Chapter One
Jace

His life was a perfectly conducted orchestra. It had to be. He needed order and control. A schedule. Jace didn't like surprises. He didn't like it when things didn't go the way he'd planned. He was beta to one of the only true shifter wolf packs in North America. And they were growing in size every time one of his wolves decided to knock up their mate.

Dom and Corey had a four-month-old baby girl named Hadley. Linc and Maddi were pregnant. She was due in the fall. And although they hadn't told anyone yet, Baze and Pen had found out last week that they were finally expecting.

With every new announcement, Jace's concerns multiplied, growing along with the girls' ever-expanding waistbands. Baze may have been pack alpha, but Jace worried over their chosen family as much, if not more, than Baze did.

Jace was an eighteen-year-old guy whose idea of a good time was checking all the security cameras before going to bed. The ones at the house where he lived with Baze and Pen, as well as the ones he'd secretly installed at everyone else's homes. He could never be too careful, and he didn't fuck around when it came to his pack's safety.

Anyone with half a brain could tell he was this way because of his childhood. Jace had grown up with a monster as his only parent, and it showed in everything Jace did. Insult to injury, four months ago his father had tried to kill him and everyone he loved. His home had been invaded by men armed to the gills who had shot at his friends, his family. There had been explosions, blood, and lots of destroyed furniture. They'd hidden the girls in Jace's safe room, and he truly believed that was the only reason no one he cared about had been injured.

In the end, his pack had won. But that didn't make the situation any less tragic.

"Hey, bubs, your brother is pulling in through the gates." Penelope stepped out onto the patio, a sweet apologetic smile on her face. "I wanted to give you a heads-up." She sat on the end of the lounger Jace was in, her hand going to his shin.

Pen was Baze's mate. They'd reconnected after ten years apart during all the drama and turmoil with Jace's father who had used Pen as a weapon, trying to force their pack to react without thinking. It hadn't worked. Instead, Pen seemed to cement everyone into their roles, making them stronger. She'd shed intense light on shifter culture and life, telling them things that they never knew. She'd been the one to point out that Baze was their alpha and Jace their beta.

"Thanks for the warning." Pen knew he didn't like it when people showed up unannounced to their home. "He's the fucking worst."

"He's your brother, and he loves you." She shook her head, chastising him in the warm way that Jace would only ever accept from her.

At the first sign of his father's impending attack, Baze and Jace had forced the whole pack to move into Jace's mountain compound. There was safety in numbers, and having them spread over the St. Leasing campus would have been a juvenile mistake. After they'd defeated Franklin, Baze and Pen stayed with Jace when the rest of the pack had gone back to their respective homes. Jace had asked his alpha to move in permanently. Jace didn't think he could have returned to a life where he was always alone.

"He *loves* to be a pain in my ass." Jace grinned, tightly, showing her he was only half kidding.

"You boys are going to have to start watching your language." Pen shook her head as she rubbed her palm over her still-flat stomach. "This family is about to be overrun with toddlers, and they can't learn words like fuck, shit, and damn before they learn to say momma."

As Jasper stepped out of the still open sliding glass doors, Jace kept his smile and his eyes trained on Pen as he addressed his brother. "Please go the F away."

She snorted, patting his knee and getting to her feet. "Good job, bubs."

"*Go the F away?* Really? How 'bout, fuck no." Jasper crossed his arms over his chest, receiving a swift pop to the side of the head from Pen on her way back into the house. "Dude, come out with us tonight."

It was normal for Jace to be annoyed by *any* interruption because that was who he'd been raised to be. Controlled. Focused. Mechanical. Humanity still baffled him. But at the moment, his brother was interrupting the one small moment of peace he'd carved out for his afternoon. And when he said carved out, he meant he'd actually fucking scheduled it.

Pen, on the other hand, could never interrupt his peace. She only ever brought it.

"I'm taking back your key." Jace relaxed back against the cushion of the lounger and closed his eyes, hoping Jasper would take the hint and leave him be. "This doesn't constitute an emergency any more than last week when you were out of beer and the stores were all closed."

Jasper, his twin in looks and blood only, lived in town with their friend Riley.

"Running out of beer in the middle of a party is *always* an emergency." He sensed his brother walking forward, then sitting in the glider next to him. "And you would know that if you ever bothered to have any fun."

"What are you talking about?" Jace frowned in annoyance. "I let you drag me to a party a few weeks ago."

"That was three months ago, lame-ass."

His eyes popped open. "For real?" Had it really been that long since he'd gone out with his friends? He could have sworn he'd suffered through a crowd of drunk teenagers only last month.

"Yeah, it was toward the end of baseball season. We won that intense game against Sacred Heart and you rode to the field with Riley so you didn't have a choice but to come with us." Jasper shook his head in mock despair. "You've gotta get that stick out of your ass, bro."

Jace straightened in his chair, reaching for the table to grab his cup of hot lemon and honey tea. "I don't have a stick up my ass." Right before he could bring the drink to his lips, Jasper knocked it out of his hand and sent it sailing into the lush green grass of his yard. "What the fuck, man?" He clenched his fists, fighting the immediate urge to punch his brother in his smirking face. Corey, Dom's mate and his counselor, had him working on his "responsive violence."

And Jasper tested it, constantly.

"You're sitting on your patio on a Friday evening in the middle of summer, sipping fucking *tea*." Jasper stood, then squatted down and dumped him out of his lounger before Jace could react to stop him. "I can't let you live like this, man, I can't."

Jasper let the chair fall back to the deck with a thud and then held his hands out in a halting gesture when Jace jumped to his feet and moved to charge him. "You're my brother and I love you. But you need to spend a little time acting your age before it's too late."

Jace ground his molars, still seriously considering coldcocking his twin. "So you think coming over and pissing me off is the way to get me to do what you want?"

"Well, man, I've called and texted. I've tried to coax you as best I could, but that shit doesn't work with your stubborn ass." Jasper stepped up to the back door, opening it and then sweeping his arm wide to gesture inside. "Get changed, and let's go have some fun before we're too old and gray to enjoy it."

Jace did not feel like partying with his brother and their best friend Riley. Going out sounded loud and exhausting, not to mention messy because drunk teenagers tended to spill a lot. But it'd been three months since the last time they'd forced him to spend time with people his own age. If he did this with them tonight, he could reasonably deduce he wouldn't have to do it again. Ever.

Riley and Jasper were starting college in three months, which meant they'd be too busy and too far away to come over and hassle him. They'd both been accepted to the University of Northern Colorado to play ball, and the campus was two hours away. Which meant they'd never bother to drive down here for a townie party.

"Fine." He knocked Jasper's hand away when he held it out for a victorious high five. "But we're calling a driver, I'm not going to be stuck at this party waiting on your drunk ass to get done hooking up with some random whore so I can drive you home."

"Works for me." He chuckled as he spoke, "But dude, it's twenty nineteen. You can't call chicks who enjoy sex *whores*."

That was a valid point: although his brother did have a certain proclivity for bedding girls who were unavailable. He and his twin had gotten into their first real fight because Jasper had fucked a chick with a boyfriend. It'd caused drama and Jace had reacted without thought, doing the only thing he knew to stop Jasper from shifting in front of a bunch of humans and revealing their thousands-of-years-old secret.

He'd beaten him until he was unconscious.

All that seemed like it'd happened a lifetime ago. But in reality, it was a mere two years in the past.

"All right, fucker." Jace put a smile on his face that he didn't feel. "Let's go have some fun."

Jasper grinned like he'd handed him a billion dollars and the secret to life. Jace turned on his heel, heading up his floating staircase to get changed for this godforsaken party. If him going out and drinking a few beers made his twin that stupid happy, then it was the least he could do.

After all, Jasper had killed their father for him without blinking.

Chapter Two
Axie

She wrapped her hair around the scalding-hot curling iron, then pulled it straight to make sure her locks cascaded down her back in waves and not ringlets. It was Friday night, and she had a party to get to. It would be the same people, the same drama. But what was the alternative? Stay in and run the risk of seeing her father?

No fucking thank you.

Three more months in this stupid town and then she'd be free. She'd been accepted to the University of Nevada the middle of her senior year and to date, it had been the happiest day of her miserable life.

She set her curling iron down on the marble countertop, grabbing a stack of beaded bracelets and sliding them up her wrist.

Sure. From the outside looking in, Alexandra Contreau had a picture-perfect existence. The big house, the wealthy family, the formidable father. She had a closet full of the most expensive clothes a girl could want, and a car that would make most people drool in envy. But to her, it was all tainted since it came at a price she was no longer willing to pay.

Axie moved from her bathroom to her large walk-in closet, searching through her collection of tight dresses. It's not as if there would be anyone at the party that she wanted to impress. She wasn't sure why she was wasting her time looking for the perfect outfit.

She rolled her eyes at her own pathetic routine before blindly grabbing a short red sundress off a black velvet hanger and pulling it down her body. She knew what guys saw when they looked at her: long legs, a rack a bit over a handful, and a face many described as beautiful. Not bragging, but she knew all the boys she'd gone to school with would give their left nut to have her. And to be honest, more than a few of them had.

But that was all before. When she was still playing the game, still distracting herself.

As she stepped into a pair of nude wedges, her bedroom door flew open. Her father felt the need to make an entrance, no matter how few people were around to see it. Maybe it was his shifter nature, or maybe he was just a pompous asshole. She used to think Miguel Contreau was larger than life. But over the years, he'd shrunk to be less than human.

Always, petty and reaching.

"Alexandra, good, I caught you before you left." His tone was as crisp as his linen suit that didn't have one single wrinkle in it. He refused to call her anything other than her given name, and he always scrunched his nose in disgust when anyone called her Axie. "I need to speak with you."

She straightened, tossing her hair out of her way as she grabbed a studded leather clutch off her ornate antique vanity. "Yeah, well, better luck tomorrow."

As she went to step past him, he grabbed her arm, pulling her back into her room. His grip tightened to the point of pain, and it took every ounce of strength she had not to let it show. Instead, jaw clenched, she steeled her spine, slipping a haughty mask over her face. Her sheer defiance was in her stance, even when she kept quiet.

"You *will* listen to me, and then you will follow my instructions to the letter." He shoved her down onto her bed, and there was no way to look collected as she landed hard. "I have word that Jace Franklin, Franklin's son, is at the party you're no doubt on your way to tonight."

Franklin.

She'd heard than name nonstop her whole life. Her father had always referred to the insufferable asshole as a "work associate." But she wasn't stupid, not anymore. She knew her father did more than defend criminals in the courtroom.

"Yeah, and what does that have to do with me?" She knew that Mr. Franklin was a bad guy, like she now knew her father was as well. And as far as "associate" went, she was pretty sure the term he was actually looking for was *frenemy*. Franklin was the boss and her father had always been jealous of the large, bald, sexist prick.

When she was little, she hadn't minded seeing Franklin. He was never outwardly mean to her. In fact, unlike most men, he'd ignored her. She'd liked it. She'd liked that he didn't watch her, didn't make her feel uncomfortable in her own home. But as she'd gotten older, the more attention she paid to her surroundings and the people who came and went from her house, she realized something: Franklin ignored her because he hated women. They were beneath him. And that simply wouldn't do for her.

She'd started being rude, going out of her way to piss him off. Eventually, her father started banishing her to her room when Franklin would come over for dinner or meetings. It was probably for the best. Franklin looked like a cold-blooded killer. And if she was going to die for her defiance, she wanted it to be worth more than some off-hand feminist comments.

"Well, my dear *daughter*, it has everything to do with you." The way he said daughter made it sound like a dirty word. "I want you to get close to Jace. I want you to watch every move he makes. I want to know if he's planning to take over in his father's absence."

Absence? That sounded like he was away on a tropical vacay. Franklin was dead. Super dead. Shot in his barrel chest dead.

And now her father wanted to know if Jace was on his way to becoming the newest boss, making him her father's newest competition. She knew he believed he had worked too long and too hard kissing Franklin's ass and playing the good little soldier to not get to take his place.

Mash all that shit together, and she could easily see that she wanted absolutely nothing to fucking do with what he was asking of her.

Axie got to her feet, smoothing the nonexistent wrinkles from her dress. "Yeah, no thanks." She held her chin high, moving past him once again.

And, once again, he grabbed her arm in a bruising grip and jerked her back to stand in front of him. "You *will* do as I say." He smiled, looking a lot like the Grinch. "You will do whatever it is that girls like you *do*, and you will pull him in. You will learn his plans, you will learn everything about him. And if you don't, I'll put a stop on the large check I just made out to UNLV this afternoon."

She froze, her heart pounding inside her chest so hard she was afraid it'd be visible. She vowed to never let her father see any of her weaknesses, but apparently, she'd failed at some point. He knew that getting out of Haxton, Colorado, was the most important thing in her life. She'd spent more time studying lines of coke in a mirror over the last four years than she had studying in a textbook. Which meant her father had needed to make a sizable donation to get her into UNLV.

She knew she should be ashamed because she knew that his check had probably been signed in someone else's blood. But she'd do whatever it took to get out of this house, away from her father and the life he wanted for her. And somehow, she'd shown him how to hit her where it hurt the most.

Axie loathed that she needed his money to get away, and hated that he held it over her head like a guillotine. Miguel Contreau had never allowed her to have a job. That would have given her an opportunity to stand on her own two feet. He'd made her dependent on him, on his dime. If she did run away, he'd chase her, find her, and punish her for defying him. He didn't love her. No way. He'd stopped caring about his daughter the day her mother died. Axie was a possession. An instrument he could use at his whim. If she wanted out, she had to make it look like she wasn't running.

Nevertheless, Alexandra Contreau was never one to take a beating lying down.

"I'll do my best." Her tone was hard, her jaw tight so she didn't spew her hatred and defiance all over his crisp white shirt.

Her father nodded, like he'd won. "Jace is controlled. He's regimented and smart as a whip. He's calculating, and he was raised to be a leader. In short, he's absolutely nothing like you." His gaze traveled down her red dress. "So, try not to act anything like yourself." He released her and she wanted so badly to rub at the pain that radiated through her arm, but of course she would never. "Sit pretty with your mouth closed and he should take the bait."

She felt her dinner start to make its way up her throat. She shouldn't be surprised by anything at this point, but for some reason the fact that her father wanted her to use her body to drop a guy to his knees made her feel physically ill.

"Sure thing, *Daddy*." The way she said that last word had the same amount of disdain as when he had said daughter.

She stepped past him, out of her room and down the curved sweeping staircase. She walked out the front door, hands shaking, using every ounce of willpower she had left not to slam it. She wouldn't give her father the satisfaction.

She would never let him know how much he hurt her.

How cheap he made her feel: how insignificant.

He didn't deserve her help or her compliance. She didn't understand why he would want her to stay in Haxton, punishment or not. She was a thorn in his side. She made his life difficult every damn chance she got. But even if his threat had been an empty one, the idea of being trapped here had rattled her all the same. So, she'd lure the clueless Franklin clone in, sure. But she wouldn't pretend to be anyone other than herself. And she'd get *just enough* information to keep her father busy over the next two months.

Then she'd be gone, and she'd never glance back.

Chapter Three
Jace

Jace was leaning against a brick wall, a beer bottle dangling from his fingertips. He'd let his brother drag him to some public school house party in town. There were drunk humans dancing, drinking, and dry humping all over the place.

It was comical, if not disdainful.

The large red brick house was full of lights and people, loud music, and a thick cloud of weed smoke. There were probably girls doing coke in the bathroom, and someone was no doubt getting blown in a bedroom upstairs.

It was teeth-clenchingly cliché.

But Jasper seemed downright giddy, and Riley was having fun. And that was the only reason Jace was here. He'd grown up alone, without any laughter or physical affection. But he'd missed his twin constantly. He'd never admit it out loud, but he would do anything to make sure Jasper was happy. He never wanted his real or chosen family to feel one ounce of the emptiness he'd felt as a child. It wasn't something he'd wish on his worst…well, that simply wasn't true. He'd wish that and more on the people who set out to hurt him and his.

Jace scanned the backyard, searching out signs of danger automatically. It had been ingrained in him from a young age. Always be vigilant. He'd stalked his own father as a small child, gauging his moods and his comings and goings. Anticipating the next beating that was headed his way. If he could brace himself, prepare himself, then it seemed to hurt less.

Being caught by surprise was one of his biggest fears.

"You know, more people might come speak to you if you removed that murderous look in your eyes." Riley came to stand beside him, trading out Jace's lukewarm beer for a cold one.

Jace put the new bottle to his lips and took a deep drink. "Yeah, but then I'd have to make small talk with these assholes and that seems like the worst way to spend a night."

Riley chuckled, leaning his back against the brick. "Why'd you agree to come, man? You hate this shit."

"Jasper spilled my tea and dumped me onto my back porch." He sighed, showing his utter exhaustion. "It was either come to the party or punch my twin in his smug face."

A guy stumbled past them, leaned over, and retched into the kidney-shaped pool. He crawled to his feet, high-fiving one of his buddies as he weaved his way back to the keg.

"I'm guessing right about now, you're wishing you would have punched Jasper instead?"

"Completely." He nodded, his nose wrinkled in disgust at the vomit slowly sinking into the otherwise clear blue water. "Absolutely."

"Did I hear my name?" Jasper came over to their place in the shadows, his shifter eyes seeing them clearly when not many others could. "I'm assuming you're cussing my ass right now?"

Riley smiled, his baby face and freckles making him look younger than his eighteen years. "Of course he's cussing you, bro." He threw his arms wide, encompassing the juvenile party taking place in front of the three of them. "You dragged him into his worst nightmare."

That was slightly dramatic, if not a little bit accurate. Jace didn't like parties. He didn't like being surrounded by strangers. He didn't like the way these humans celebrated their loss of control the way they did. It was as if total stupidity and self-annihilation was the goal.

But he supposed, if he viewed things from his twin's perspective, he could see the appeal. There were girls running around in dresses so short you could see their tight young asses. And all of them had hungry gazes trained on Jasper and Riley. Even their human eyes could see that there was something altogether different about his twin and his best friend.

And those young women wanted to experience what that difference felt like.

"It's only his worst nightmare because he refuses to fucking participate." Jasper shook his head, like he was disappointed. "You need to get laid more than any man I've ever met, bro."

"Leave him alone, Jasper." Riley shook his head, a warning in his tone. "That's not something you should try to force him to do. It's not right."

Riley was kindhearted, tender in a way that few shifters were. He cared about people, about their feelings. The night Jace had opened his mouth and spilled his secrets, Riley had been understanding and kind. Jasper had laughed and promptly called a group of girls. He had them sneak onto the St. Leasing campus then helped them climb up into their dorm room. He'd presented them like gifts and Jace had gone into the bathroom and puked his guts up.

Jace was a virgin, and he had piles of reasons as to why.

But Jasper didn't care. His twin thought it was something he needed to rid himself of, like pulling off a BAND-AID or the scab on a long-healed wound.

But the wound wasn't healed, and he wasn't sure it ever would be.

"One more word out of *your* mouth about *my* dick and I'll hold your head under that vomit-filled water until you pass out." Jace turned to look at his twin. "Then I'll step over your body and go to bed with a damn satisfied smile on my face."

"Graphic, bro." Jasper sighed, taking a sip of whatever vile substance was in his red Solo cup.

Riley put a hand on each one of their shoulders. "Hey, at least he threatened to make you only pass out. That's a big step up from murder, so we're making some real progress, guys."

Jasper chuckled at Riley's joke, but Jace stayed silent.

They stood in a row drinking their beers and watching the party escalate in front of them. They didn't move, seemingly content for the moment in their companionable silence. That was until a girl in a short red dress stepped into their line of sight.

The dress she wore was short, like all the other girls' dresses. But hers was flowing around her body, moving when she did like a stream of water made of silk. Her hair was long, dark, and wild, giving her an exotic look that worked well with her deep green eyes and smoky makeup. She was gorgeous, but Jace could tell by the way she moved that she knew it, and that was a strike against her.

Riley dropped his bottle, the glass shattering on the pebbled pavers. Jasper pushed off the wall, taking one step toward her like it had been an automatic response. And Jace did nothing. He stayed perfectly still, his head cocked to the side, studying the girl who had instantly captured his brother's and friend's adoration.

She was searching for something, someone. Her gaze moving around, never stopping to notice any of the guys who were working hard to gain a moment of her attention. Her small purse was being twisted in her hands like she was apprehensive, but her face maintained an almost flirty smile like she was trying to keep anyone from noticing her worry. She bit her bottom lip every few seconds, and the wind was carrying her sweet floral scent to his shifter senses.

Jasper took another step in her direction, his arm extending like he wanted to snatch her from the crowd and drag her away and into the shadows with them. Jace found that he was okay with that. He wanted her to be missing from everyone else's gaze. He wanted to hide her here with him in the dark. Every male in the vicinity looked at her with nothing but lust and desire in their eyes.

And it was making him feel shifty.

"Holy shit." Riley shook his head, like he was trying to clear the fog in order to think more clearly. "That's the hottest chick I've ever fucking seen." He was whispering, like he was afraid he would spook her if he spoke any louder. "I think I'm—"

"Dibs." Jasper shoved Riley back against the brick wall, cutting him off and stepping into the light before quickly making his way through the throng of people.

"Fucker." Riley sighed, resuming his place beside Jace with an irritated scowl on his face. "She's gorgeous." They both watched as Jasper introduced himself, taking her small hand in his. He pulled her closer and she laughed lightly at whatever he'd said. "That prick better share."

Jace swallowed past the lump that formed in the back of his throat. His pulse had started to race and his mouth felt dry. He wanted to rip out Riley's throat so he wouldn't be able to say another word about her, he wanted to cross the patio and shove his twin into the disgusting pool. He wanted to throw that girl over his shoulder and carry her all the way to his home, then never let her leave his sight. Or his bed.

But it wasn't her beauty that was calling to him. It wasn't her green eyes or her sinful body that was making Jace start to lose his ever-present control. It was something else. It was something that couldn't be seen with his eyes.

It was something that he felt down in his soul.

And it fucking terrified him.

Chapter Four
Axie

On her way to the party, Axie had done a little stalking. Living with her father had taught her one thing: know thy enemy. So she knew what Jace Franklin looked like. Although there weren't many pictures attached to his social media, she'd been pleased at what she would get to see in person: a dark-haired, dark-eyed Greek god. Maybe seducing the guy would end up being a good time after all. He had muscles on top of muscles, but a lean build, like he was carved out of granite. He seemed tall, standing a few inches above most of the people in his photographs. He had a straight nose, a jaw that was sharper than glass, and lips that most girls would pay good money for. No smiles in any of the snaps. She was sure she could help with that.

The guy currently hitting on her was nothing like the man her father had described. This dude was forward and was blatantly propositioning her. He was quick with a laugh and his eyes danced with the dirty thoughts running through his brain. He didn't seem controlled or regimented at fucking all. He seemed juvenile and childish, like a frat boy gone rough.

She cut off his latest attempt at flirting, "I'm sorry, what did you say your name was?"

She was almost positive he'd told her when he'd barged into her personal space and taken her hand, spinning her in a playful circle. But she'd been too distracted by the fact that she'd spotted her prey so quickly to pay attention to his words.

"Jasper." He kissed the back of her hand and she fought the sudden urge to wipe it off on his jeans. She wasn't a prude, far from it. But for some reason, the guy smiling at her... He didn't *feel* right.

He looked like the photos she'd seen of *Jace* Franklin, so much so that her mind was having trouble rectifying the fact that he wasn't the person she'd set out to find when she arrived. She opened her mouth to ask if he was using a fucking alias, but then her eyes landed on two people watching them from the shadows.

They were standing against the brick wall of the large house, taking in her interaction with this Jasper character. One of the guys had floppy red hair, and he looked like he belonged in a high school baseball dugout, not here in the middle of this drunken debauchery. The other? Well, the other was exactly who she'd been searching for.

Franklin had two sons, twins. Did her father know that? Did anyone? Although, now that she had both in her line of sight, she saw they didn't look exactly alike. There were small differences that made them stand apart.

"Are those your friends?" She couldn't tear her gaze away from the *real* Jace, and he was staring right back. But his attention on her body wasn't lustful. He wasn't planning out all the things he wanted to do to her in the dark. He was studying her, observing her like *she* was the prey. "Can I meet them?"

Jasper glanced over his shoulder. "Oh, uh, yeah, sure." He seemed disappointed by her request, but she wasn't here to kiss hurt egos. This party had become a means to an end. The moment her father had entered her room, this party had changed from a break from reality to the key to her escape.

Jasper put his hand on her lower back, dangerously close to her ass. She wanted to shove him away, but she didn't want to piss him off and lose her chance to meet his penetratingly serious twin brother.

"This is my best friend, Riley, and my brother, Jace." Jasper's hand was still on her, and she stepped closer to Jace to get away from the unwanted touch. "Guys, this is…I'm sorry, I didn't catch your name."

He didn't catch it because he hadn't asked. They both knew that he hadn't cared what her name was. It hadn't been important. He'd spotted her the moment she'd stepped foot into the backyard and he'd *wanted*.

Blind and simple lust.

"Axie." She smiled at Riley and he started to blush, endearing him to her in a way that she didn't think her jaded heart was capable of experiencing. She moved her gaze to Jace, taking in his rigid stance and his clenched jaw. Controlled, calculated, exactly as her father had warned. "Nice to meet you."

She watched as Jace finally seemed to snap out of whatever trance he'd been in, letting his gaze travel down her body and back up again. Then he cocked his head to the side, appearing a little like a deranged serial killer. Except she wasn't afraid. Quite the opposite. She'd have been intrigued even if her father hadn't tasked her with getting close to him.

This guy was dangerous in a way her body craved. Jace Franklin didn't care who she was, and he didn't seem to give two fucks about what she thought of him. There was no spoiled air about him. He wasn't holding court, throwing his weight around. He was hiding in the shadows like he was hoping no one would notice him.

"Axie, can I get you something to drink?" Jasper's hand was on her lower back again. "What's your poison?"

Dark and dangerous apparently.

"I'll take whatever whiskey they have, neat." She didn't drink beer. It was beneath her. Wine gave her a headache, and vodka made her a little crazy. She honestly could have gone without the drink, but she wanted Jasper's touch off her body. Normally, she didn't mind guys like him, thinking they had a chance and not being able to keep their hands to themselves while they awaited her final decision. But tonight, she could barely stomach it.

Perhaps because her father had basically tasked her with prostitution.

"Boys? Anyone need another?" Jasper pointed to Riley and then Jace, his eyebrows up in question.

The cute redhead nodded, tossing his empty across the yard, sinking it into a trashcan. Was he showing off? That shot would have been impossible for most of the boys here to make.

"Jace?" Jasper looked pointedly at the beer dangling seductively from his twin's fingertips. Why did she find his hold on the bottle so fucking sexy?

"Sure." His *voice*, holy shit his voice. It was as dark as his gaze, rough and deep, rolling over her in waves that seemed to shake her to her core. "Riley, go with him."

Jasper waved away his twin's suggestion. "He can stay here, keep my new gi—"

"Riley." Jace kept his eyes on hers as he cut off Jasper, speaking Riley's name as if it was a command. "Go with him."

His tone brooked no argument. Riley and Jasper both walked off like puppies with their tails between their legs after having been commanded by their alpha.

Jace appeared to be every bit the presence her father had made him out to be. He'd yet to smile, and aside from appraising her like she was an item to size up, he didn't seem interested in the least.

She found herself stupidly holding her breath, wanting to know what he thought of her. Did he like what he saw? Did he want to know more about her? Was he drawn to her, like she was to him? Jace Franklin unnerved her, but she was used to feeling uncomfortable in her own skin. She'd learned at a young age to hide it well. So she didn't wither under his glare. She held her head high. She returned the favor, perusing him, doing her best to make him feel he too was as much under a microscope. Axie would always give as good, if not better, than she got.

"Why did you send him away?" Her voice sounded breathy, even to her own ears. "Didn't want the competition?" She was trying to throw him off, find a chink in his armor.

"We both know there is no competition, Axie." He spoke quietly, calmly, like he had all the time in the word to let his words roll off his tongue.

His arrogance was showing, reminding her of his father in that moment. How was Jace to know that she wasn't interested in anyone else at the party? She hadn't acted in a way that would give him that idea. He couldn't read minds. He couldn't know that she'd loathed Jasper's touch and immediately placed Riley in the adorably handsome friend zone.

No, even shifters couldn't infiltrate senses like that.

She decided to brush off his cocky comment, and look for another way to knock him off his high horse. "You look out of place, standing stoic in the middle of a party." She glanced over her shoulder, jerking her head slightly to the crowd of drunk dancers getting closer to the edge of the pool with every song. "You want to dance?" She would bet her life that he would turn her down. Jace Franklin did not seem like the dancing type.

His kept his dark eyes on hers, his lips twitching like he was possibly contemplating a grin. She couldn't tear her gaze away, silently willing him to keep going. She wanted to see what the devil looked like when he smiled. But before she could get her answer, Riley and Jasper interrupted, and a drink was thrust into her hands. It was a heavy glass tumbler, not a red plastic cup, which she had to appreciate.

She took a sip, humming in appreciation at the warm amber liquid. She let her tongue dart out to taste her bottom lip, making sure her eyes stayed on Jace. "So, what'll it be?" She was goading him, and they both knew it.

Jace shook his head slightly, like he couldn't even be bothered to make the full gesture. "Dance with Jasper," he answered, a dare in his deep tone. He was calling her bluff, upping the stakes of the game they'd started to play.

Axie didn't back down, ever. It wasn't in her DNA.

She threw the room temperature alcohol back, tilting her head and exposing her throat on purpose to three young shifters. She was teasing them, tempting. She was showing them her weakness without a shred of trepidation. She was letting Jace know that she wasn't scared of him. That she didn't fear him.

Jace didn't react. Did he even realize that she knew who and what they were? Or did he think she was a simple public school human? She didn't have a dick, so she hadn't been welcome at St. Leasing. But that didn't mean she was clueless.

Her father was a ruthless shifter, like Jace's father had been.

She turned a seductive smile on Jasper, taking his hand and pulling him along as she walked backward onto the dance floor.

Checkmate, motherfucker.

Chapter Five
Jace

Jasper was pressed against Axie, curving his body around her until there wasn't an inch of space separating them. Jace could see the lust in his twin's eyes, the anticipation in his smile. He thought she was his for the night. That he'd gotten exactly what he wanted.

But he was so fucking wrong.

Jace felt pulled to her like there was an invisible thread tugging him in her direction. His hands itched to shove Jasper away from her, demand that he never put his hands on her ever again. He wanted to grab her arm and drag her away from all the guys here who were dreaming of fucking her. For the first time in his life, he felt possessive, and he couldn't say he was happy about it.

He clenched his jaw, draining his fresh beer before tossing it across the yard into the trash like Riley had earlier. He needed to get the hell out of there. He needed to get away from Axie before he did something stupid. He wanted to run away from the tightness in his chest and the grasping jealousy rushing through his veins. He refused to listen to the voice screaming inside his head, the one repeating the same damn word over and over again.

He was stronger than this.

He was stronger than fate, than his instincts. He could fight…he *would* fight. He had to. Axie couldn't be his. He'd promised himself a long time ago that he'd never have a weakness. And that girl, smiling into the shadows at him as she let his clueless twin run his hands all over her sinful body, was exactly that.

A fucking weakness.

"I'm out." He pushed away from the wall, pulling out his cell to call the driver they'd used to get to the party a couple hours earlier. He didn't turn to tell Riley good-bye: he couldn't. He needed to leave. He needed to put distance between him and the girl in the red dress. He hadn't touched her, even though he'd wanted to…so fucking badly. If he left now, maybe he could save them both.

As he walked across the dark yard, the beat of the music and roar of the crowd faded into a whisper and he felt himself start to relax. The tension in his shoulders lessened, the muscles in his jaw loosened. He took a deep inhale, allowing himself his first full breath since he spotted Axie.

Headlights shone in his face, making him close his eyes momentarily. His escape was here, another few seconds and he'd be safe. The car slowed to a stop, and he opened the door, refusing to wait for the driver to put it in park. He felt panicked, rushed, completely unlike himself. And he loathed it.

"Leaving so soon?"

The voice behind him was mildly sarcastic, and it shot chills straight down his now-rigid spine. He put an expressionless mask on his face, one that he had perfected years ago. He only half turned to face Axie, refusing to give her his full attention. "Nothing here worth staying for."

He wanted to wound her. He wanted her to hate him.

But instead she smirked, tsking playfully. "Now, we both know that's not true."

This fucking chick. Why couldn't she leave him alone? What did she want with him? He was telling her he wasn't interested, so why was she still trying? There was a guy back at that party, with his same face, throwing himself at her feet. And Riley would no doubt be game to join in for good measure.

"If it wasn't true, then I wouldn't be leaving."

"Ouch." She said the words he wanted to hear, but he knew the emotion wasn't real.

He hadn't hurt her if the laughter in her eyes was any indication.

"Good-bye, Axie."

He climbed in the car, slamming the door, refusing to let himself look back.

Chapter Six
Axie

Well, that had not gone according to plan. She hadn't even let him see her wild side, her chaos. She'd unintentionally followed her father's orders, and had been relatively well behaved. Yet Jace still walked away like she didn't matter. And now she was feeling a little bit reckless. It wasn't her fault really. She hated being dismissed, being treated like she wasn't important. It'd been happening her whole life and it was a bit of a trigger for her.

She couldn't be held accountable for anything that happened from here on out.

Females didn't shift, didn't have the DNA anomaly. But she was still born of a shifter, and she was pretty sure it played a part in her personality from time to time.

She stepped back into the shadows where Jasper had been waiting after she'd left him on the dance floor, and began running her hands up his muscular chest. When they'd been dancing, she could barely tolerate his hands gliding along her body. But it wasn't as hard to touch him now that his twin was gone, and she chose not to examine that fact too closely. "You guys ready to have some real fun?"

She cut her eyes to Riley, a seductive gleam in her gaze. Jace didn't want to play? That was fine. She'd let the two guys still here distract her instead.

Axie took one of each of their hands, holding them high above their heads as she danced her way into the house. People waved hello, but she didn't stop moving. The party inside was crowded and full of smoke and noise. The music was so loud it was hard to discern the lyrics. The bodies were packed so tight that she had no real way of knowing who'd grabbed her ass as she moved into the hallway. She knew the bathroom in the master would be empty, because she knew they kept that bedroom locked during parties like these.

But she also knew where they kept the key.

She dropped the guys' hands, stood on her tiptoes, and ran her fingers over the top of the doorframe, smiling when she felt what she was searching for. She unlocked the door, dropping the key into the cleavage of her red dress for safekeeping. After Riley stepped over the threshold, she locked the three of them inside the spacious bedroom. The walls were light beige, the bed large with fresh seafoam green linens. She kicked her wedges off, knowing from experience that this master had the lushest carpeting.

She left Jasper and Riley to look around and headed for the palatial en suite. She took the clutch that had been hanging from her wrist, opening it and dumping the contents on the marble counter. She needed more than the whiskey. She needed something stronger.

Axie wasn't happy about Jace's brush-off. It affected her more than it should have, and she was having trouble shaking the deep-seeded rejection she felt coursing through her veins.

She wanted to be numb. And lucky for her, she always came prepared.

She unfastened the lid of a small black metal box, and using a matching minuscule spoon, she scooped out some of the white powder. She pulled a blade from the lid and began to cut three lines. She didn't need Jace. She had his friends. She didn't need Jace's attention to make her feel good. She had drugs for that.

Axie had learned a long time ago that she was the only person in charge of her happiness.

"Boys, come play with me." She snorted her line, loving the instant rush taking over her senses. She no longer felt dejected. And she was well on her way to feeling fucking fantastic.

Jasper came in, wearing his seemingly permanent smile. She wasn't sure what it would take to make him lose his jovial attitude. But tonight wasn't the night to find out. "You got party favors, doll?" He glanced from the cocaine on the counter to her and back again. She held up the rolled Benjamin in her hand, a dare in her eyes.

She wanted to party, and she needed them to participate.

Jasper took his hit like it wasn't his first time, and for some reason that made her feel excited, made her feel less alone. Maybe he was like her, maybe he needed an escape. He turned, passing the bill to Riley.

Now that poor guy looked less than pumped about the cut good time she was offering him. But maybe he wasn't really grasping what else went along with it. She put her chin on his shoulder, kissing the side of his neck, enjoying the sight of her lipstick on his skin. "Come on, kid, have some fun with us."

He surprised her by snaking his arm around her waist and putting his mouth against the shell of her ear. "I can have plenty of fun with you without the coke." He ran his nose up the column of her throat. "But we both know that we aren't the ones you're craving right now."

Riley's whispered words threatened to derail her newfound high.

"Who fucking cares?" Jasper dipped down, taking the third line himself and then quickly putting everything away and shoving it back into her bag. "The girl wants to party, let's fucking party."

Jasper grabbed her hand, spinning her out of Riley's hold and pulling her back into the dark hallway while she was still trying to shake Riley's comment. She glanced back once, making sure that he was following them back to the dance floor. She needed the cute redhead to stay with them, which made no sense to her. He'd called her on her shit. He knew she was using them as a placeholder for a guy she'd barely shared a conversation with.

Jasper on the other hand? He was game for anything and everything she was willing to do. Luckily, the coke was blocking whatever had made her repulsed by his touch earlier. When he twirled her around on the crowded dance floor in the living room, she reveled in the feeling of bodies pressed against hers. She wanted the contact. She wanted to be unsure of who was where. She wanted the confusion and the bliss to mix together until all of her thoughts disappeared. She wanted Jace's twin and their friend to make her forget she'd ever met him.

Jasper was grinding against her ass, Riley in front of her with his fingers in her hair. She didn't know these shifters, but at the moment she really didn't fucking care. They were exactly what she needed, and she was thankful for them.

They were stronger than the human guys she was used to, their touch rougher and altogether unapologetic. Jasper and Riley operated in sync, working her body over like this wasn't the first time they'd had a girl between them. Riley trailed his hands down the column of her throat, his palm on her exposed sternum pushing her tighter against the guy behind her. She felt Jasper's hard length pressed to her lower back, his fingers digging into her hips. The three of them moved together, the deep hypnotic beat of the music drowning out all rational thought.

Fuck you. Jace Franklin. He and her father could suck a dick for all she cared.

Axie put her arms in the air, letting her hand pull at the back of Jasper's neck. She needed more. She needed his mouth on her heated skin. He chuckled against her bare shoulder, his voice barely audible above the pounding bass. "You want to get out of here, doll?"

Before she could open her mouth to say yes, Riley grabbed her face in one hand. Her eyes flew to his to see him shake his head, an impassive expression on his baby face. He didn't want her to leave with them? His rigid dick grinding against her stomach told a different story so she wasn't too sure where his hesitation was coming from. Was it Jace? Was it because he thought she wanted someone else?

She rolled her eyes and spun around, wrapping her arms around Jasper's neck. Riley could go suck a dick with Jace and her father. She stood on her toes, licking the shell of his ear. "Take me away."

Jasper trailed his fingers down her arms, threading them through her own. His playful smile now looked a little wicked. Good. She didn't want nice and polite. She wanted to be owned. She wanted someone else to anchor her to the earth, if only for one night.

Coke always made her feel a little crazy, a little disconnected. But this was something altogether different, something *more.* Her skin felt flushed, feverish. Her pulse was rapid and she couldn't seem to take a full breath. She was horny. There was no other way to put it. She wanted someone's body on top of hers. She wanted someone inside her. She needed to feel full, and she needed to come.

Jasper took her hand, unwinding her from around his body, moving easily as the crowd parted for them like they were royalty. She let him lead her, more than happy to go wherever he was taking her. He wouldn't hurt her. There was no need.

She'd give him exactly what he was after.

She glanced behind her, curious if Riley was going to follow or simply stand there and pout about the fact that she'd ignored his command.

He wasn't hurrying, and he didn't look pleased, but he was making his way through the throng of people.

Before she knew it, the sound of the party was muted and the three of them were standing out at the end of the long gravel driveway. Riley had his phone up to his ear. They had a driver? Perfect, she wouldn't need to call hers to come shuttle them wherever the hell they had planned to take her.

Maybe they should go to her house? She could parade Jasper past her father, up the stairs, and into her bedroom. She'd lock the door, and she'd scream Jace's name as she came. She doubted her father would even bat an eye. Hell, she'd probably get a raise in her allowance.

"This isn't going to end well, you know that, right?" At some point Riley had stepped closer to her, dipping down so that his face was level with hers. "Let me call you a ride home, Axie."

She kept her eyes on his, refusing to look away as she shook her head slowly. Riley didn't understand the need clawing at her insides. He didn't know that she couldn't go home, not alone anyway. If she didn't find relief, if she didn't connect with someone, she was pretty sure she'd die.

Jasper wrapped his arms around her waist, putting his mouth back on her shoulder. "You're so fucking hot, doll face."

She closed her eyes, enjoying the feel of him pressed against her. Enjoying his smile against her skin, the way his words made her want more of it all. She dropped her head to the side, moaning when she felt his teeth scrape her flesh. *Yes.* That was exactly what she was searching for, that dangerous line between pleasure and pain.

"Don't fucking bite her, man." Riley's warning was spoken low, like he was trying to be stern with two children. "You know what happened with Jace tonight, you *know* what that was."

Jasper rested his chin on her shoulder, his hands gripping her hips so hard that she knew she'd have bruises in the morning. "If that had been the case, he'd be here right now, wouldn't he?" He laughed, his breath tickling her mercilessly. "But he left. She chased after him and he *left.*"

Riley fired back, "Of course he fucking left, wouldn't you?" She was starting to get more than a little irritated with their side conversation. Wasn't the coked-out horny chick supposed to be the center of attention? She opened her eyes, a shudder wracking through her body.

"You two are killing my buzz." She stood up straighter, sighing as she tried to shrug Jasper away from her neck. They were more than killing her buzz. They were making her so cranky she was starting to feel sick to her stomach.

"No, *I* wouldn't have left." Jasper kept his grasp tight on her while speaking over her head. "Fucking look at her. I'd have been on my knees thanking the universe and worshipping this girl like she was my own personal god."

Well, that was flattering, and a little bit confusing.

Maybe she needed more coke. They'd ruined her high and their driver was taking too long. She was starting to lose that lustful feeling that had been burning through her body a few minutes ago.

She stepped away from Jasper, no longer enamored with the feel of him pressed against her ass. He didn't get the hint. Instead of letting her go he held her tighter. She opened her clutch, taking out her little black box. A bump should fix this situation right the hell up.

Riley and Jasper kept arguing with each other, not even seeming to notice that she'd put more powder up her nose. It was okay, because in a few minutes, she'd be back to not caring about anything. Including the two warring shifters she was captive between.

Axie tilted her head back, smiling up at the stars and resting her back against Jasper's hard chest. He took that as an invitation to put his mouth on her skin once again. She didn't love it as she had before, but thanks to that last hit of coke, she didn't hate it either.

"Can't you feel that? Can't you feel the lust in the air? It's palpable." Jasper scraped his teeth along the muscles between her neck and shoulder. He groaned, his hips thrusting against her ass. "Fuck, man. I want her so fucking bad." She felt him open his mouth and her pulse started hammering in response.

Her eyes flew open at the sudden wrongness of it. *Wait.* What was happening? Fuck. She didn't want *more* like she had before. No.

She wanted him to stop. He had to stop. She didn't want his teeth on her. There wasn't enough coke in the world to make her want that.

She opened her mouth, fully prepared to scream.

But she never got the chance.

Chapter Seven
Jace

Jace made his twin bleed, again. But this time, the little asshole had wholeheartedly deserved it.

Riley had called Jace. And when he had answered the phone, Riley had whispered that they needed a pickup, for *three*. Jace knew what Riley had meant, and it had taken him less than six seconds to decide that he wasn't about to let it happen.

He'd made the driver turn around, and demanded the little fucker break every speed limit on the way back to the party. Then Jace had him park the car around on the other side of the house, his curiosity fully prepared to damn him to hell. He moved through the woods, listening intently to the argument that Riley and Jasper had been having, making sure Axie had no clue what was transpiring over her head.

When he'd stepped into the clearing, Riley had his fists clenched at his sides with a resigned expression on his face. There was no need for him to explain what was happening when he'd spotted Jace moving out of the trees.

Riley had known Jace's reaction to Axie meant something important, and he was pissed Jasper was willing to ignore it in order to get his dick wet by a coked-out girl who seemed up for anything.

Jace stopped, standing a few feet away, watching his brother put his hands all over Axie. He studied the girl and his twin, feeling the instant she started to panic. The instant her body recognized that *his* was close again, and everything inside her reacted to his nearness. She was appalled by Jasper's touch, and she'd even opened her mouth to scream.

He'd been more than content to let her too, but then his brother had fastened his mouth around the flesh at her neck, and Jace lost his fucking mind.

She wasn't Jasper's to mark, to take, to play with.

"You could have stopped after he went down." Riley brought Jace back to the present, from his seat across from him in the extended black town car, checking Jasper's vitals.

Jace knew his friend was right, but he hadn't really been in control. No, hitting his brother until Riley had managed to pull him off was all instinct. The same instinct that had Axie pressed up against his side right now.

She was shaking, and she refused to look at him. Or even acknowledge his presence. But she still sought him out, inching nearer until the only way she could get closer would be to climb into his fucking lap.

"What's she on?" He was speaking to Riley, gesturing with his head to the girl practically vibrating next to him.

"*She* is right here." Her teeth seemed to be chattering, so he took off his button-down and laid it over her like a blanket.

Which served two purposes: she'd be warmer and it would mask some of Jasper's scent that was still lingering on her skin and pissing him the fuck off.

"Okay, *Axie*, what are you on?" He'd humor her, and if she tried to lie to him, he'd go back to speaking about her like she wasn't there.

"Coke." She shrugged like it wasn't a big deal, which irritated him to no end. He ground his molars together so he didn't tell her as much. A lecture wouldn't help anything right now anyway. "And the whiskey from earlier."

"Can't handle your high very well, now can you?" He was being condescending, but he couldn't seem to help it. He was disappointed in her choices, in the fact that she'd let Jasper touch her, kiss her. He didn't like the jealousy he still felt, he didn't like any of what was happening tonight.

He felt out of control.

"I can." She had a sharp edge to her voice. "But those two started arguing, which killed my fucking buzz." She seemed to give up the fight of resisting the warmth he'd offered as she put his shirt on. "So, I took another hit."

He rubbed his temples. This night was giving him a monster headache. Riley and Jasper arguing wasn't what had dampened her high, but how was he supposed to explain that right now? She was a ball of nervous energy. Jasper was bleeding all over the leather upholstery, and Riley looked supremely disappointed in the lot of them.

"You need to go home and forget you met any of us." He spoke to her softly, wanting her to hear the honesty in what he was saying. "It'll be the best thing for you." And for him, but she wouldn't understand what that meant.

Sure, he'd suffer, but he wouldn't die. Baze had proved that theory a million times over with Penelope. It would hurt, and he'd be miserable. But he would live, and she'd be safe and that was all that would matter to him from this night on.

He'd known who she was the moment he'd laid eyes on her. And about two seconds after that, he'd decided that he'd never act on it. He'd never claim his mate, because that life wasn't in the cards for a guy like him. His life would never be entirely his own, he'd never be completely right. No one deserved a mate like him.

She opened her mouth, presumably to argue with him. But luckily, they were pulling up outside of her house. He leaned over her lap, opening the door. "Good-bye, Axie."

He knew that her body would be demanding she stay next to him, like his was crying out in protest at her departure.

"I kn—"

"Good-bye. Axie." He unbuckled her seat belt and all but shoved her out the door. The second he could slam it closed, he yelled to the driver to *drive*.

He didn't take a full breath until he wouldn't have even been able to see her if he'd wanted to punish himself by looking out the rear window.

"He wasn't hurting her, she wanted him." Riley was slumped in his seat, his head in his hands. "He wasn't forcing her to do anything. He could sense her lust and—"

"And it wasn't for him," Jace finished. "I was watching her. The second her body sensed mine, she froze. She was seconds away from screaming bloody fucking murder."

Riley dropped his hands, resting his elbows on his knees. "So why'd you go after him? I was right there, I would have made sure he let her go."

That was all probably true. "I couldn't stop myself." That right there though, was the *truest* statement he'd ever uttered. "Thank you for calling me. For watching out for her, and for pulling me off him."

"Why'd you leave in the first place? What was your endgame, pushing her into his arms?"

He sighed, leaning back into his seat, getting comfortable for the drive back up the mountain. "I don't want her."

Riley chuckled, the sound not holding much humor. "Could have fucking fooled me."

"I *don't* want her." He wasn't lying. "And I thought maybe if I could get out of there, I could pretend that I'd never laid eyes on her. I could pretend that my wolf hadn't noticed that sexy girl in the red dress."

"Sexy?" Riley snorted. "Dude, you have no fucking clue. When we were dancing with her in the living ro—"

"Unless you want to be passed out next to Jasper, I suggest you don't finish that fucking sentence." He shook his head slowly, making sure that Riley understood the thinly veiled threat. Jace didn't want her. He'd never claim her as his. But that didn't mean he could handle hearing about her wedged between his twin and his best friend.

"What now?" Riley rested his palm on Jasper's chest, which was probably to make sure he was still breathing. "Running away didn't do shit, you came right back and all but killed Jasper."

"I go into my own house and face the fucking firing squad." The car had stopped in front of his double front doors, and it'd taken him about thirty seconds to notice all the other vehicles in the driveway and all the lights on inside his home.

Riley held his hands up, like he was trying to keep Jace calm. "I called Baze, giving him a heads-up on what we were bringing with us. I never expected him to activate the damn phone tree."

Jace was irritated and exhausted. Now he was going to have to explain himself to his alpha, and worse, the girls.

"What are you going to tell them?" Riley leaned forward, opened the car door, and stepped over Jasper's body to get onto the concrete. "What excuse could you possibly give them to explain this?" He reached back inside the car, picking up Jasper, who was already in a healing sleep.

"The truth." Jace climbed out of the car, slamming the door and watching as the vehicle turned around and headed back to the gated entrance. "Jasper got all coked up and lost his fucking mind for a minute."

Chapter Eight
Jace

Okay, so maybe his version of the truth wasn't completely accurate. Lying by omission to his pack didn't feel great. But he also wasn't about to fucking tell his chosen family that he'd kicked his blood brother's ass because Jasper had deemed himself worthy to touch *Jace's* mate.

Not a fucking chance.

Jace had all but pushed Axie out of his car *and* his life. He didn't need weaknesses. He didn't need distractions. A mate was never in his life plan. Even though his instincts had been screaming at him, he hadn't touched her. Which meant he hadn't started to bond, right? The person who would be able to tell him for sure was also one of the people who could never know. So. That sucked giant flaming dick.

"Oh my god, Jace." Penelope threw the door open wide, making room for him and Riley to drag Jasper inside his home. "What the hell happened?" She pulled the silky teal robe with a pale floral rose print tighter around her slim body. Jace had given it to her on her birthday.

He moved past her, not answering her question. He wasn't sure he could look her in the eye and straight up lie to her. Pen was Baze's mate, but she was also his favorite person on the entire planet thanks to the mate-sharing crap alphas and betas went through.

"Again, man. Really?" Linc shoved him out of the way and helped Riley get Jasper comfortable on the couch in the main room. "This is not the way I wanted to spend my night, kids."

Jace stepped back away from his pack as they all gathered around his twin, fussing over his bruised and battered body. He swallowed thickly as he made his way to the vintage glass bar cart next to the large stone fireplace. He needed something stronger than the weak-ass beer he'd forced down his throat at that shit show of a party earlier.

He poured himself three fingers of the single malt scotch, tossing it back like it was nothing more than a cheap tequila shot.

"What happened?" Baze had his hands on his hips and a pissed-off expression on his face. "Why'd you kick his ass this time?"

This time. Like it fucking happened every damn weekend or something. It'd actually been a long time since Jace had used his fists to teach his brother a lesson. Which was a fact he was pretty proud of considering how much the douche tended to dance on his last nerve.

Jace glanced around the room, taking inventory of who was glaring at him and who was missing. Corey wasn't present, no doubt at home with her and Dom's sleeping infant but cussing his ass from a distance. Maddie wasn't here either, which was good because she was a really moody pregnant chick.

"It wasn't Jace's fault." Riley spoke up from his spot at the head of the couch. "Jasper got messed up, got a little handsy with a chick who wasn't into it."

Jace had to force his jaw from dropping open. That look wouldn't be on par with his cool and calculated demeanor. Why was Riley helping him? Riley and Jasper were thick as thieves, had been since they were kids. If anyone was an outsider in their friendship, it was Jace.

"Did he, like, assault someone? Is that what you're saying?" Dom dropped into one of the dark leather armchairs, scrubbing his hands down his face. "What was he on?"

"Uh, booze and too much coke if I'm being honest." Riley crossed the room, moving in front of the bar cart and helping himself to a drink. He shot it back like Jace had done minutes before, his back to the room while he gave Jace a small resigned shrug. "The girl was all over us, and then she was over it. He probably didn't even notice the change in her. He was too wasted."

"That's no excuse." Pen shook her head, crossing her arms over her noticeably larger chest. "He deserved to have his ass kicked." She stepped to Jace, putting her hand on his cheek and making him feel guilty as fuck with the soft kindness in her gaze. "You did the right thing."

The right thing.

That was a fine line, like a tight rope he was currently walking. Riley had told a fucking close version of the truth, in true Riley fashion. Jasper *had* done too much coke, and he *hadn't* noticed the way that Axie's body had suddenly stiffened in his arms. But Jace knew that Riley wouldn't have let things get out of control. Jace hadn't needed to pounce on his twin and knock him unconscious with a swift right hook. Axie had been about to scream, and Jasper would have jumped away from her like she was on fire.

Jasper wasn't a bad guy. He'd never intentionally push a female. Right?

And letting the pack think that he was an asshole made Jace feel like the worst kind of person. The worst kind of shifter. The worst kind of brother.

"He didn't notice." Jace cleared the heavy guilt from his throat. "Jasper would never hurt anyone on purpose. She was coked out, drunk on expensive whiskey. Her reaction time was slow, and Jasper couldn't see her face."

His jaw clenched at the vivid memory. The way her body had gone rigid, the way her mouth had opened to scream seconds before Jasper's teeth had grazed her skin. His fists tightened at his sides and he had to turn away from his twin, the sudden urge to hit him again overtaking all his senses.

"You guys can go." Riley picked up the crystal decanter and poured Jace another drink. "I'll stay with Jasper until he's awake." He shoved the tumbler into Jace's hand, forcing him to loosen his fist. "It looks worse than it is."

Jace sipped the amber liquid this time, letting the warmth spread through his body and dilute the anger he still felt.

Once everyone left, Pen gave him another hug, making him feel like a hero instead of the prick he was. Baze clapped him on the back, which was pretty much a huge declaration of love between alpha and beta. He didn't deserve their kindness. He didn't deserve Riley's help either. What he did deserve was for Jasper to wake up and kick his ass all over the damn house.

"I didn't need you to lie for me." Jace left Riley standing by the fireplace and sat in the armchair Dom had vacated.

Riley snorted. "I think what you meant to say, asshole, is thank you." He took the other chair and set his drink down on the small table between them. "And I didn't lie, not really."

Riley was right, he *should* be thanking him. But he couldn't seem to make himself do it. "They can't know about Axie."

Riley nodded, taking a small sip on his new drink. "I heard you in the car, man. Doesn't make sense to me though."

"I don't want a mate."

"Who the fuck does in the beginning? You aren't special." He gestured toward the stairs. "You think any of the coaches wanted to become whipped bitches? You think they wanted to change every single fucking aspect of their lives? They only think about the girls now." He shrugged. "But they seem pretty damn happy to me."

"She'd be a weakness." Jace's father had never taken a true mate. He'd been careful to limit his interaction with females for that reason. Well, that and because he thought females were utterly beneath him. "I'm beta, I need to be strong for our pack."

"You really sitting here telling me that Pen makes Baze weak? That Molly, Corey, and Maddi make us weak?" Riley shook his head. "You don't actually believe that. I know you don't. I've heard you talk about how strong the girls are. Pen has taught us so much about our pack, about our culture. Corey made us a family. She brought us all together. Maddi is tough as nails, and Molly is all heart. We need them. We need every single one of them."

Jace knew logically that Riley was right. But he also knew he needed to be on guard, he needed to put his pack first. He needed to protect the people he loved. He'd already almost lost them too many times to count. Just because Franklin was dead didn't mean all threats were null and void. The pack didn't understand: they couldn't. They hadn't grown up around dangerous men the way Jace had. Franklin was one criminal in a sea of evil men.

"Axie is chaos." Jace got to his feet, moving over to the couch to peer down at his sleeping twin. "She's reckless, which means she's dangerous." He pulled a blanket from the basket Pen had placed on the side of the couch after she'd moved in. "I don't have the time or the inclination to tame her." He covered his brother. "The universe made a mistake."

"And what if you're the one who's wrong?" Riley propped back, kicking his feet up on the coffee table, making Jace itch to shove them down to the ground where shoes belonged. "What if you aren't meant to tame her? What if she's meant to make you wild?"

Jace shook his head on the way up the stairs. "Stop letting those chicks fill your head with fairy tales, man."

***

What if she's meant to make you wild?

A little later, Jace lay on his bed, his hands resting on his stomach as he stared up his stark white ceiling. He couldn't seem to get the image of Axie out of his mind, even when his eyes were wide open. Her dark hair, her curves: the way her body looked in that fiery red dress. The perpetual smirk on her face and the constant dare in her eyes. The moment she'd stepped into his line of sight, his whole body had reacted.

For a moment in time, he'd wanted to take the small hand she was offering him. He'd wanted to throw caution to the wind and let her body move against his on that crowded dance floor. He'd wanted to be the one making her laugh, the one making her feel desire. He'd wanted his hands on her hips, his lips on her flesh. He'd wanted to claim her, he'd wanted the whole fucking world to know who she belonged to.

But like he'd said, the universe had made a mistake.

Chapter Nine
Axie

What in the actual fuck? Axie sat up in bed, clutching her head, cursing the coke she'd put up her nose and the liquor she'd poured down her throat. Hangovers were the cosmic punishment, and she'd earned her fair share. But last night hadn't been entirely her fault.

Her father had pimped her out, dangling her freedom in front of her face like a bright orange carrot. And then her mark, for lack of a better word, had dismissed her. *Twice.*

The first time he'd walked away from her like she meant less than nothing. And the second? He might as well have shoved her out of his car while it was still moving.

Jace Franklin was exactly the man her father had made him out to be. Cold. Calculated. Detached.

His twin on the other hand…that kid was a fucking ball of personality. It was as if the universe hadn't doled out their characteristics correctly. They'd given Jasper too much and Jace too little.

Axie grabbed a pillow, shoving it over her face to keep the sunlight away. She had a splitting headache and she knew that it was only going to get worse. Her father would track her down soon enough, wanting a progress report like she was one of his soldiers and not his daughter. And what could she tell him? She got fucking high as a kite and made out with the wrong Franklin?

Jace had pushed her into his brother's willing and waiting arms with a sinister smirk on his handsome face. She'd been into it at first, She remembered craving Jasper's touch, she remembered dancing with him and Riley. Moving between the two of them, their hands roaming over her like they knew how to *share*. She'd wanted their mouths on her. She'd welcomed the distraction.

Until she hadn't.

Her breath caught in her throat as the rest of the night came rushing back to her. The way Jasper had started to feel all wrong. The argument he'd gotten in with that adorable Riley kid. The way she'd started to panic, the queasiness she'd felt as his teeth grazed her skin.

And the moment Jace had swooped in, saving her. He'd pulled Jasper off her, and he'd knocked him out. And then he'd lost his serial killer-ish mind. Jace stayed on top of him, delivering blow after blow, like he was punishing his twin for something.

Had Jace been jealous? That couldn't be it. It made no sense. She'd basically thrown herself at him, and he'd left her at that party, making it clear she was of no interest to him. Hell, she'd chasing after him like a damn puppy. And he'd still turned her down. If he had wanted her, he could have easily had her, so jealousy made absolutely no sense.

The moment she'd noticed Jace Franklin watching her from the shadows, she'd been turned on. There was something about the way he studied her. It was like his gaze was a caress, teasing her until she was right on the edge of falling. Axie wasn't new to lust. But the feelings Jace stirred in her were altogether…more.

If was almost as if—

"It's noon, Alexandra." Her father threw her door wide, stepping into her room like he was the fucking ringleader at a three-ring circus. "Please tell me you're still in bed because you were out late getting to know our new friend."

Ew. Was he really insinuating what it sounded like he was insinuating? Could he be any more fucking vile?

"I was out late, sure." She made the wrong fucking Franklin connection, but whatever, an in was an in. "I met him, we talked, we made friends."

"And did you find anything out?" He was towering over her, his arms crossed over his chest. "Did he mention his father?"

They didn't get much of a chance to chat, what with him blowing her off left and right. But she couldn't tell her father what took place last night. His head would no doubt explode, shooting his stupid brains all over her bedroom walls. She sat up, her head swimming. "Um, he has a twin brother. And Jace is every bit as calculated and tough as you said he'd be."

"Twin? Are they working together? I was always under the impression that his other son wasn't in the picture anymore."

Jasper was definitely in the picture. She'd had an up-close look herself. "They seem close." They partied together, that had to count for something, right?

"You'll be seeing Jace again?"

She tossed her covers aside, putting her bare feet on her plush rug, wanting more than anything for her father to leave. "Yes." She lied through clenched teeth, more than willing to say whatever it took to end the conversation.

"When?" Her father was now strolling around her room, studying the artwork on the walls and the old framed photos of her mother like he'd never noticed them before.

"Today." Another lie. "I have plans with him and his friends." Axie wasn't stupid, and she knew how to use what god gave her. Jasper had been more than interested, and Riley seemed like he enjoyed her company for the most part. They were her opening, and she'd take it. If nothing else, at least she could have some fun and get out of the house and away from her father's watchful eye.

"Try to dress a little less like a whore this time." He spun to face her, his hands clasped behind his back. "Jace took the bait like I'd hoped, now show him you have a little class." His nose wrinkled, like he found his own daughter disgusting. "Men like Jace Franklin only let sluts into their beds, not into their lives."

"Yes sir." The way she said it sounded more like *fuck you* and the look in his eyes told her he knew it.

He left her room without another word and she fell back onto her mattress, staring up at the ceiling and fighting back tears. She wouldn't let them fall. Her father didn't deserve them. He was her captor and financier, and Jace was her ticket out of Haxton, Colorado. They were both a means to an end, and she'd never let them get her down. She was stronger than anyone had ever given her credit for, and she could survive the next couple of months. She'd survived over eighteen years in her gilded cage. She wouldn't bow down now, not when she was so close to being set free.

She could use her connection with Riley and Jasper, she could gather scraps of information, embellish them a little and buy herself some time.

Axie plucked her phone from her charger, opening her social media app and searching for Jasper Franklin. She came up empty, confused and seriously doubting that a cocky guy like him wouldn't have an account when his stoic twin did. She scrolled through Jace's friends list, easily finding Riley and typing out a message.

@AxieC: Hey, it's Axie, from last night. Did you guys make it home okay? I wanted to check on Jasper after the ass kicking he got. Seemed brutal.

She sat her phone down, about to head into her bathroom for a long hot shower and some headache meds, when her message alert dinged loudly.

@Riley.300: He lived. We're about to head into town for some lunch, want to join us?

@AxieC: I just dragged my hungover butt out of bed. Can I meet you guys in about an hour?

@Riley.300: Sure. Send me your number and I'll text you the address.

Axie typed out her number before tossing her cell back down onto her bed and heading to her en suite. That was easier than taking candy from a baby. She thought maybe Riley would've been a little standoffish after the way the night ended. She'd planned to give her best flirt over text, entice him over to her side. But instead, he'd instantly extended an invitation. Perfect. Looked like she hadn't lied to her father after all.

Axie turned on the shower, the temperature as hot as she could stand it. She stood underneath the spray, letting the stream of water beat down on her shoulders. She felt stiff, sore, like she hadn't slept comfortably in her insanely expensive bed.

She used one hand to knead at her flesh, stretching and pulling her muscles, trying to find some relief. She closed her eyes, instantly overrun with images of Jace. The way his gaze felt, the harshness in his eyes. The way his body seemed coiled to react, finger on a hair trigger. The way his mouth looked, forming the words to blow her off. The muscles in his arms and forearms as he beat his twin. The way his jaw clenched and unclenched in a pattern when she was sitting beside him in the car.

She took a deep breath, her mouth watering as she remembered how good he'd smelled in the small confined space. She hadn't been able to get close enough. She'd wanted to climb into his lap and feel his lips move against hers. She'd wanted his cock against her core. It'd taken everything she'd had to stay in her seat.

But now, she was alone, assaulted by memories of their brief time together. There was no one around. There was no one to relieve her ache. There was no one who could see her as she let her hand slide down her heated skin, cupping herself between her legs and jerking at the contact.

Thinking about Jace was turning her on more than any porn she'd ever watched.

What was it about him that was making her lose her damn mind?

Chapter Ten
Jace

Jace woke up as pissed off as he'd gone to bed. Pissed at himself, at his twin, at the goddamn universe. Jasper had been drunk and high. But he didn't deserve to have his ass kicked like that. Jace should be able to exercise more restraint. For fuck's sake, he was the beta of his pack. He'd been raised by the coldest, most calculated man in the world who had made sure Jace had learned how to shut down his emotions.

But Axie took away his control.

Jace had been intrigued, confused, followed closely by lustful, then he'd ended up somewhere around fucking livid. She'd smiled at him. She'd teased him. She'd gotten his brother high as shit. She was a wild card, and she knew it.

At first glance, Axie seemed to be everything he wasn't. She was messy and reckless, she was indiscriminate about who she trusted her body with. She didn't appear to have a shred of self-preservation. Axie had dived headfirst into a wolf's den and she didn't have a fucking clue.

It was his shifter that seemed to rule when she was around, and that simply wouldn't do.

"Hey, I come in peace."

Jace sighed, hanging his head for a moment at the sound of his twin's weary voice. "You shouldn't have touched her like that." He set his coffee down, the glass clinking against the granite counter. "But I shouldn't have kept hitting you after you passed out, and for that, I'm sorry."

And that was the only thing he'd apologize for, because he still couldn't get the image of Jasper's teeth grazing Axie's shoulder out of his brain. And every time he thought about it, he started to get angry all over again.

"That's fair." Jasper moved across the large kitchen, making himself a cup of coffee, adding cream and caramel. "Riley tried to warn me, but I was too far gone to listen."

Jace studied his brother, watching him as he took a sip of his drink and then winced before adding more caramel. His bruises had healed overnight. All trace of Jace's fists and anger were gone, like the whole thing had never happened.

"Yeah, what the fuck was that about? Booze and coke. I don't think getting drunk and high around a bunch of shithead humans is the right way to be spending your weekends." Jace would never condone anything that lowered inhabitations like that. It was dangerous, and a good way for their secrets to be revealed to the masses.

"What?" Jasper's eyebrows rose, his hand paused with his glass mug halfway to his mouth. "It wasn't the coke that was making me crazy, man."

"I find that difficult to believe." Jace leaned back, crossing his arms over his worn black t-shirt.

Jasper stepped forward, setting his coffee down on the island. "It was *her*. It was Axie."

Jace's heart began to pound inside his chest, hearing her name come from his brother's lips. The same lips that had kissed her, had touched her flesh. He wanted to tell him to shut up, but instead he clenched his jaw, wanting more to maintain his calm exterior.

"She's gorgeous. There is no disputing that. And her body is downright fucking sinful. I can't even begin to tell you how good she felt in my arms. She was warm, and sultry. I don't know if I've ever used that word in my life. But that's what she was. She was sex, in the perfect package." Jasper paused, rubbing at the stubble on his lower jaw with a wistful look in his eyes. "But it was more than that. The need I felt when I was next to her, it was like I was in a trance. I couldn't stop touching her. I wasn't in control, my shifter was."

Jace swallowed past the large lump that had formed in his throat. His chest was tight and his whole body felt coiled to fight. But still he remained silent.

"I don't know, man. I've never felt like that before." Jasper shrugged. "Maybe she's mine. That's what it's like, right? You have to touch them, you have to claim them for your shifter to take—"

"She's not yours." Riley stepped down into the kitchen, casually breezing past them to grab the juice out of the fridge like he was walking in on a conversation about something as trivial as the weather.

Jace felt some of the tension leaving his shoulders, his neck. Riley had snapped the thick rage he'd had building inside him with his interruption. The kindhearted redhead had inadvertently saved Jasper from another ass kicking.

"How would you know?" Jasper rolled his eyes, resting his hip against the island. "You the expert on bonding? I don't think so. You're as single as me and fucking Rocky over there." He gestured to Jace, making light of the fact that his twin had beat him to a pulp only hours ago.

"Expert. No. Observant. Yes." Riley downed a tall glass of OJ, then rinsed his cup in the stainless steel sink before continuing. "Axie didn't want you to touch her. It was written all over her face. The second you started to bite her, she panicked."

Jace growled, then covered it up like he was coughing when both Riley and Jasper swung their eyes his way. He pounded at his chest. "Coffee went down the wrong pipe."

Riley scoffed, but Jasper let it go. "So she didn't want me to bite her, maybe she was just confused. I'm sure no other dude has ever tried to mark her on night one." He chuckled at his own joke, but no one else was laughing. "I can't explain it, man, I was so drawn to her."

"She didn't want you to mark her, and you tried to do it anyway." Riley shook his head. "If she was *yours*, you would have stopped. Don't you get it? If she was meant to be your mate, you wouldn't do anything she didn't like. You'd never hurt her. You'd never scare her. Your shifter wouldn't let you." Riley glanced at Jace. "The reason you were drawn to her is simple, it's the same as when everyone was drawn to—"

"It was the coke." Jace stood abruptly, the metal legs of his stool scraping the wood floor. "It's not good for us, for our kind. Don't fucking do it again."

He'd known what Riley was going to say, he'd known where he was headed. Jasper had been drawn to Axie the way they'd been drawn to Maddi before she'd bonded fully with Linc. Axie was near her mate, and her body was begging for the connection. That's what

Jasper had been feeling, and what had started to drive him crazy. His shifter had taken control, not because she was meant to be his, but because she was meant to be someone else's.

"Whatever you say, fun police." Jasper hopped to his feet, speaking across the island to Riley. "You ready for lunch?"

Riley was staring at Jace, his eyes communicating everything he wasn't saying out loud. Jace gave him a slight shake of his head, the movement almost too small to be real. He didn't want anyone else to know. He wanted Axie to disappear from all their lives, he wanted last night to never have fucking happened.

"Yeah, man, let's go." Riley broke his eye contact with Jace, stepping around the island to the door that led to the front of the house. The one he'd had to replace after it'd been shot in by his father's men.

Jace stood, watching them as they left his home. The home he'd purchased in order to protect them all, to protect his pack. It'd been instinctual. He'd done it without true thought. Jace, the secluded boy who grew up without love, opened his home to everyone he cared about. And that included his twin, and their best friend.

But if he found out Jasper fucking touched Axie one more goddamn time, he'd kill him.

Chapter Eleven
Axie

She'd showered, and she'd touched herself with her eyes closed and Jace's face burned into her brain. God, the way he'd studied her. He was gorgeous, dark and brooding. She didn't know if he'd ever laughed in his whole life. That was the vibe he had, indifferent, always. But her body had reacted to each little thing about him.

And now, she was walking into lunch with his twin and the adorable redhead with the floppy hair. Why? Because she needed some intel to share with her father to get him off her back. And she'd damn well get it over a giant cheeseburger. She was still feeling hungover as shit. Maybe the grease would help.

"Hello, boys." She put a big smile on her face, making sure her eyes danced as she let her fingertips graze their shoulders. "How's everyone feeling this morning?" She sat down at the small dark wood table, hanging her bag on the made to look old metal chair.

"Never better." Jasper grinned, winking at her as he leaned forward in his seat. "You?"

She shrugged, drawing attention to the loose-fitting shirt hanging off one shoulder. "I woke up with a killer headache, but the giant burger I'm about to eat should help." She picked up the menu, searching the list of sides. "And some onion rings."

She looked across the table, making sure her easy smile stayed in place. She wanted more than anything to ask about Jace. She wanted to know why he hadn't come to lunch. She wanted to ask if he was still mad at Jasper. She wanted to know if they'd made up.

But that wouldn't get her where she needed to be.

"I'm a bit of a bad influence, huh?" She pouted, knowing how enticing her bottom lip would look to them. "Sorry if I got you guys in trouble."

Jasper waved away her concern. "It's all fun and games, right?"

She laughed lightly. "Isn't there more to that saying? Until someone gets hurt?"

"Do either of us look hurt to you, gorgeous?" Jasper leaned forward again, his forearms pressing on the plastic-covered menu.

She dragged her eyes across each of them playfully. "No, I guess not."

If she was human, she would have questioned Jasper's lack of bruises. She would have wondered if she'd dreamed up the beating he took last night. But she wasn't altogether human, and she wasn't sure why they couldn't see that.

Last night in the car, Jace had warned her away from them like he was trying to protect her. But she didn't need protection. She needed information.

"Well, before your psycho twin lost his shit, I was having a great time." Her gaze moved between the two men sitting in front of her. Jasper was smiling, but Riley's eyes narrowed slightly, his lips forming a thin line. He wasn't buying a word she was saying. But the question was, why?

"You have plans tonight, gorgeous?" Jasper brushed his leg against hers under the table.

She shook her head. "I'm all yours."

Axie should have felt guilty for using Jasper to get information about his brother. But this was her life, her freedom. And she couldn't afford to have a conscience.

***

Lunch hadn't gotten her much intel on Jace Franklin. Every time she tried to bring him up in conversations, Jasper would change the subject. Finally, she gave up. Her head was still pounding, and she didn't have the energy to keep trying to do her father's bidding. Besides, Jasper had asked her if she had plans that night. She could try again later.

They'd finished eating and their waitress had cleared the empty plates moments before. Now Riley had his phone out, his fingers flying across the keyboard. And Jasper had his hand on her thigh under the table.

She wasn't repulsed at his touch, but she didn't welcome it either. It felt wrong, but she couldn't really explain the reason why. Not in a way that would make sense anyway.

"Riley. You got somewhere else you need to be?" She smiled when he finally glanced up from his phone.

He grinned back, setting his phone down on the table. "Actually, yeah, Jasper and I have to head to campus for a bit."

She picked up her soda, taking a long sip. "I thought you guys graduated this year."

"We did." Jasper resting his arm along the back of her chair, leaning closer to her. "We're helping our coaches get the varsity roster ready for fall training." He spoke proudly, like he enjoyed helping the team.

"You know, I've been to a few St. Leasing games over the years. I'm sure I've seen you both on the field." Her school played them every season, and every season they lost. They weren't in the same division: it was more of a fundraiser friendly rivalry type game.

"Well, I know I've never seen you at a town party before." Jasper used his thumb to caress the back of her neck. "I would have remembered you."

Cliché flirting at its finest. Axie smiled in response, almost wishing he'd make it harder on her. Make her work for his attention. How fucked up was that?

"We gotta head out, man." Riley got to his feet, shoving his cell into his pocket. "Axie, you need a ride home?"

"Oh, I don't want you to go out of your way." She let Jasper pull her out of her seat, his hand on her lower back as he started to steer her toward the door. "I can call my driver." She laughed lightly. "I couldn't drive here. I was afraid I was still drunk." And by drunk, she meant high. But she'd never say that in the middle of a small-town diner.

Jasper put his arm around her neck, pulling her close and kissing the side of her head. "No worries, gorgeous, we can drive you home before we head to the field."

It was a kind offer, considering the St. Leasing campus was five minutes from town and her house was fifteen minutes in the opposite direction. Axie had Jasper. He was wound around her little finger. She bet if she met up with him tonight, she'd be able to pull all kinds of information from that handsome brain of his. She'd give her father what he wanted, and then she'd lay low. Maybe she'd head to Nevada sooner than she'd originally planned.

"Well, as long as it isn't an imposition." She leaned on Jasper's shoulder, all but batting her eyelashes at him. "I'd love a ride."

His pupils dilated at her flirty response.

Silly predictable shifter.

Chapter Twelve
Jace

Jace stared at Riley's text for a solid two minutes, reading it over and wishing that it didn't bother him. He closed his eyes tight, clenching his teeth, wishing it all would go away. He wanted Axie to not exist. He wanted her to stop affecting him. He wanted to turn back time and never go to that stupid fucking party last night.

Riley: Axie is meeting us for lunch, your twin is super pumped.

Jace knew that Riley was baiting him, but he couldn't exactly figure out why. What was his end game? Did he want Jace to storm into the café and toss Jasper through the damn window? And then what, grab Axie and mount her on the table? Drive into her relentlessly until he showed her and the entire fucking world who she really belonged to?

He shook his head, trying like hell to clear that image from his brain. And get his stupid dick to calm down.

"Why do you look so irritated?" Baze came into Jace's home office, taking one of the chairs facing his large desk. "Someone piss in your Wheaties?"

"Sometimes I wonder why I wanted you to live with me." Jace put his cell face down beside his laptop where he'd been watching the security cameras he'd secretly installed all over the St. Leasing campus.

Baze smiled in return, which still took Jace by surprise occasionally. Baze Carter had been a miserable hard-ass for as long as Jace had known him, for as long as he'd coached them at St. Leasing. But becoming their alpha, having his mate back in his life had softened him.

Jace being beta had only hardened him further.

"Pen wants to know if you want to go with us to our ultrasound next week." Baze and Pen were over the moon excited when they found out they were pregnant a few weeks ago. They hadn't told the rest of the pack, although Jace was pretty sure that Riley had figured it out when he was here the other day. "It's our first appointment and she's a little nervous."

"She knows we can hear the baby's heartbeat, right?" Baze and Riley were the only two in the pack who could pick up on changes that small. They'd both known instantly when Corey had gotten pregnant with Hadley. And he knew Baze knew Pen was pregnant a few days before she'd gotten that big pink positive on the pee stick she waved around the house crying happy tears. "If there was something wrong, we'd know." Over the last few days, Jace had started hearing the tiny flutters as well. And it made him smile every single time.

Baze shrugged. "You can't tell a pregnant chick anything, man."

"I'd love to go." And he would. He gave Baze a hard time, but he would be lost without him and Pen living here. He'd be lonely, and a lonely Jace was even more of an asshole than normal.

"Okay, good. Pen will be excited."

It was hard for Jace to let people in, to trust that everyone wasn't out to destroy him. But over the last few months, he'd been happier than he'd ever been.

Until Axie.

Baze leaned back in his seat, assessing Jace over steepled fingers. "Is there anything else you want to tell me?" He'd taken on his alpha tone, like he meant business.

They did this often, switching from their easy life at home with Pen to their job taking care of their pack. But for the first time, Jace had secrets that he wasn't ready to share.

Jace sighed, mirroring his stance because two could play at that game and even though Jace was younger, he'd been playing it longer. "Are you fishing? If there's something you want to know, then ask, alpha."

"You beat the ever-loving shit out of your jackass of a twin." Baze narrowed his eyes. "You're usually more controlled than that. The last time it happened, you were protecting him from Franklin. But Franklin's dead, and you and Jasper have grown a lot closer over the last year, so I have a hard time believing your story."

Baze was right, Jace and his twin had grown a lot closer. Even more so after Jasper had killed Franklin for him. True, Jasper annoyed him, forced him to do shit he didn't want to do. He drank all of Jace's expensive booze, and usually missed the toilet when he was pissing, but Jace loved his brother. His teeth on Axie was probably the only thing that could have elicited that beating. He wasn't about to tell Baze about her though. Axie needed to stay the fuck away from all of them. For his sanity, and for her and Jasper's safety.

"Jasper drank, then snorted enough blow to kill a thoroughbred. He was high, he was horny, and he was acting inappropriately. I did what I did to protect him, *again*. Or would you have been okay dealing with a sexual assault charge?"

His answer wasn't a lie, but it wasn't the whole truth, and the look on Baze's face told him he wasn't buying it.

"We both know you took Jasper out with one punch." Baze stood, resting his palms on Jace's desk. "But it sure looked like you didn't stop there. His nose was broken, might have fractured his eye socket, and at least two ribs were snapped clean in half."

Jace wasn't proud of what he'd done to his brother, but he knew he'd do it all over again in a heartbeat. Jasper's mouth, his hands, didn't belong on *his ma*...on Axie.

"I did what I did. He got the punishment he deserved." Jace stood, because he'd be damned if anyone talked down to him in his own office, even if Baze was his alpha. "If you have a problem with it, then do something about it."

They stared at each other, neither one of them giving in. Pack order dictated that Jace should back down first, and usually he would. But not when it came to this, not when it came to Axie.

"Hey, there you two are." Pen breezed into the room, either oblivious to the power struggle or ignoring it. "Did you ask him about the appointment?" She smiled at them both, that wicked grin she wore firmly in place telling Jace it was the latter. Pen could feel the tension and she was giving them no other choice but to dispel it.

Baze straightened, putting his arm affectionately around his mate. "Yes, I did, and he'd love to go." Baze glared at him over Pen's head, like he was daring him to transfer his defiant attitude to Pen. "Right?"

But there was no need. Jace would never treat her poorly. "Of course." He made his features soften as he walked around his desk to kiss the top of her head. "I wouldn't miss it for the world."

Baze playfully shoved Jace away from his mate. "This mate sharing is a pain in my ass."

Pen had been tossed into the pack during the chaos with Franklin, and she'd brought them more knowledge than they'd known what to do with. She seemed to know anything and everything about shifter life and culture. And she was the one who told them all about mate sharing between alphas and betas. Nothing physical. More like a love borne from the need of a mate-less beta to protect the alpha's mate at all costs. Baze was right, it was a fucking pain in the ass, but Jace really adored Pen.

Pen laughed. "Well, I love it." She kissed Jace's cheek before taking Baze's hand and pulling him toward the doorway. "I don't know what I'll do when you meet your forever."

According to Pen, the mate sharing would stop the second Jace bonded with his soul mate. He assured her that was never going to happen. Mostly, he did it to fuck with Baze, but also because he didn't want to mate with anyone. He wasn't meant for that life. He didn't need anyone else to worry about, to keep safe. He wasn't raised with love and affection. It didn't come easy to him. He was surly and grumpy, and serious most of the time. He'd never be able to make a mate happy.

"Come on, you need a nap." Baze was the one pulling her out the door now. "Time to rest those hormones before you get all weepy thinking about your bubs leaving the proverbial nest."

The second he heard Baze and Pen start up the stairs, Jace collapsed back in his chair, picking up his cell to type out a reply to Riley. He was going to tell him to fuck off, and then he'd make sure that he and Jasper knew in no uncertain terms that Axie was off limits. She needed to disappear from their lives, not sink deeper in.

But when he opened the text screen, a chill went down his spine. Riley had sent a picture of Axie laughing with her head thrown back while Jasper looked at her like he wanted to mount her.

Jace's fist tightened until he heard his cell start to crack in protest.

He headed for the door, grabbing his keys from the entry table as Baze was coming back down the stairs.

"Where are you going? We aren't through with our little chat."

Jace tossed a wave over his shoulder on his way out the front door. "You can ineffectively interrogate me more later. I have shit to do."

Shit to do and a twin to murder.

Chapter Thirteen
Jace

Jace had parked next to Riley's truck, then watched the three of them through the large restaurant window that faced the street. Jasper was sitting next to Axie, and Riley was across from them. They were talking and laughing like old friends. On the drive into town, Jace had willed himself to calm down. He'd gone through the facts in his head. He'd used logic and training to convince his shifter to let Jasper live.

Jace wasn't being honest with his twin. He was hiding things from him. He reasoned that if Jasper knew that Axie was meant to be his, he'd back off. Jasper had killed their father to protect Jace's soul. He certainly wouldn't try to steal his mate.

But seeing them together, seeing the easiness in the way they interacted, was making the rage return. She didn't belong with them. She was a human who didn't know the first thing about what was happening around her. She was clueless and flirting with disaster.

Jace watched as Axie put her hand on Jasper's arm. No, she wasn't flirting with disaster. She was toying with fucking chaos. He started toward the door, his blood pumping like lava through his veins. But the second he opened the door, they all stood. He paused, backing out again, suddenly unsure of himself and what he should do.

Should he let his presence be known, or did he get back in his car and drive back to the safety of his home in the mountains?

"Well, as long as it isn't an imposition, I'd love a ride."

Why was she looking up at Jasper like he hung the fucking moon? Why was his arm around her? Why had Jace driven here? What the hell had he been thinking? He hadn't. Once again, the image of Jasper and Axie together had brought his shifter to the surface.

Jace waited outside the door until all three of them exited the diner, then he stepped down off the curb, clicking the unlock button on his key fob. "Get in the car, Axie, I'll take you home."

Axie jumped, her hand flying to her chest. "Holy shit. Where the fuck did you come from?" She bent at the waist, her hand going to her knees. "You scared the crap out of me."

He hadn't meant to step out of the shadows like a creeper, but it was either that or hide like he was spying on them. Which was true, but it was beneath him and he refused to admit that's what he'd been doing. Besides, he'd be damned if he let Jasper give her a ride home.

He shrugged like her fright was unwarranted. "I had an errand in town and saw Riley's truck, then heard you talking about needing a ride home."

Jace glanced at Riley in time to see him bite his lips together like he was trying to hold in a smile. Smug bastard.

"No, man, we can take her home." Jasper opened the back passenger door to Riley's truck, his eyes narrowed in apparent confusion. He was as shocked to see Jace as Axie was. But unlike Axie, Jasper was pissed.

Jace could sense his twin's annoyance from where he was standing on the sidewalk. Jasper wanted more time with Axie, and Jace couldn't blame him. She looked gorgeous in her short shorts, her hair piled high on her head. Her sun-kissed skin was on full display, and Jace could smell her sweet scent the moment she'd walked out the door.

"No." He stared at his twin for a beat, then moved his eyes to Riley, who knew that they would drive Axie home over Jace's cold dead body.

Riley gave him a slight nod in concession before hopping up into his truck. "Come on, Jasper, we've got plans with coach anyway. If we're late, we'll never hear the end of it."

"We still have loads of time, it's—"

"Get in the goddamn car, Axie." Jace cut off his brother, his tone barely above a snarl. He hadn't meant to be such an asshole about it, but he was quickly losing his patience, and Baze wouldn't let him get away with beating the shit out of Jasper a second time in as many days.

All three of them watched as she narrowed her eyes at him, her chin lifting higher. "Excuse me?" Axie was going to refuse him, simply because she could. Jace didn't know if he should be pissed or amused with her show of strength.

He liked that she didn't bow down to him. It made his pulse start to thrum in his neck and chills spread down his spine. Her defiance was turning him on.

Jace took a deep breath before trying again, "Axie, please, get in the car and allow me to drive you home. Riley and Jasper have plans, in the opposite direction." There, maybe logic and a pleasing tone would work better.

She rolled her eyes, blowing a kiss in Jasper's direction before hopping off the sidewalk and strutting to Jace's car. Her every move seemed like she was being intentionally sexy. The smirk on her pouty lips, the sway of her ass as she got in the car, the annoyance in her eyes as she slammed the door.

Axie was made for him all right. And continuing to deny it was going to be the hardest thing Jace would ever accomplish. His shifter was restless and pissed. He wanted to be let out, and he wanted to mark her. He wanted to claim her and show everyone that she would only belong to him. Forever.

Jace got behind the wheel, backing out of the parking space with Jasper glaring at him the whole time. His brother was clueless. Or maybe he was too blinded by Axie to pay attention to everything that was happening right in front of him. Riley seemed to be attracted to her, drawn to her. But he knew better than to touch what wasn't his. Riley was observant, always assessing his environment, looking for subtle changes. But that certainly wasn't Jasper's strength.

"Thanks for demanding to take me home." Axie sent him a toothless smile when he glanced her way before focusing on the road once again. "Nothing like getting bossed around by a virtual stranger."

"You seem to be okay giving yourself to strangers, so really, what's the difference?" He was still pissed that she'd let Jasper rub his scent all over her fucking body. Riley too for that matter. It was a good thing she'd showered this morning, otherwise he might have felt so inclined to beat the shit out of both his pack mates this time.

Axie scoffed, crossing her arms over her chest. "Did you just call me a whore?"

"Don't be dense." Although Jasper had told him he needed to stop slut shaming less than twenty-four hours ago. "If you had such an issue with me demanding your compliance, then you should have told me to fuck off and walked your happy little ass home."

"Or I could have taken Jasper and Riley up on that ride."

"Wasn't going to happen." There was zero chance that Jace would have let her get in Riley's truck. There would have been a screaming match the likes of which Haxton, Colorado had never seen before.

Jace drove fast, but safely. When he'd turned sixteen, the best stunt drivers in the world had trained him. His father had wanted him to have every skill possible at his disposable. He couldn't figure out why. It wasn't because he wanted him protected in all elements. Franklin had tried to harm Jace on the daily.

His hands gripped the wheel, his knuckles turning white. He needed to get her home and get her the fuck out of his car. Her smell was intoxicating and her soft flesh was tempting him every time he let his eyes drift her way. He wanted to glide his palm up her thigh. He wanted his mouth at her exposed neck. She was calling to him, to his shifter. Like a fucking siren trying to lure him to his death.

The universe could fuck the hell off.

"So, about last night—"

"Jasper was wasted, he was taking things too far. You were panicking, so I did what I needed to do." He'd rehearsed that explanation over and over on his drive to the café. He knew eventually someone would bring it up, and he knew that he needed to blow it off as nothing of importance.

He couldn't tell her that his shifter had reacted to another unbonded male going after what belonged to him. She wouldn't understand, and he was pretty sure he'd cut out his own tongue before he acknowledged what was happening between them out loud.

Axie rubbed her hands on her bare thighs, like she was suddenly uncomfortable. "I wasn't panicking."

"Yes, you were." She could lie to herself all she wanted, but Jace had seen the look of terror in her eyes. The closer he'd stepped toward their little threesome in the making, the more her body had started to reject Jasper's presence. "But either way, it's over and done with."

"I don't need a guy to save me." She shifted in her seat, turning to face him, her eyes dancing with fire. "If I didn't want his hands on me, I could have stopped him."

Jace couldn't help the snort of laughter that left his mouth. "You would have had a better chance stopping a speeding bullet than you would've had stopping my twin." Jasper's shifter had been close to the surface, begging to come out. Jasper had wanted Axie more than he wanted air, more than he wanted to live.

She fell silent, turned to watch the forest fly by outside the window, but Jace could hear her heart racing. His words had scared her. They reminded her of the way she felt last night in the moment. Terrified and trapped.

He took the next left, slowing as he drove down the winding path that led to her house. It was massive, made of light-colored stone and cedar trim. It blended in with the forest around it instead of sticking out like a sore thumb like a lot of new builds in the area seemed to do. He'd memorized the drive last night, committing it to memory without even meaning to. Which was also part of his training growing up: to always be aware of his surroundings. His father had told him that at any moment their enemies could kidnap him, blindfold him, drive him out to the middle of nowhere. Yeah, he didn't get your average bedtime stories.

Axie took a deep breath, blowing it out and making all the wayward hairs from her topknot dance. "So, did you go to St. Leasing with Riley and Jasper?" She leaned her head back against the seat, rolling to the side to look at him. Her whole demeanor had changed, like she was reaching for casual.

He felt her gaze on his face as he continued to focus on the road, which was the only reason he didn't snarl at the sound of his twin's name on her lips. "I did. I graduated a few months ago."

"Did you play baseball too? That's what that place is all about right? The best baseball on this side of the world."

Small talk? Jace detested small talk. But it was better than her being pissed at him or lying about her every action or reaction. Plus, her house was getting closer every second, and soon he'd be rid of her. "Yeah."

"Wow. You are a great conversationalist." She laughed quietly. "Riveting."

"I went to St. Leasing. I played ball." He shrugged as he rounded the circular drive. "You're not asking the most interesting questions."

He insulted her, again. He wasn't sure why he kept doing that.

"How long have you lived in Haxton? Just the four years? Where did you live before that? What's your greatest aspiration? Boxers or briefs? Where do you fall on the death penalty?" She smiled sarcastically as he put the car in park in front of her house. "Better?"

"I moved to Haxton my freshman year, like most of the kids who go to St. Leasing. Before that? I lived in Colorado Springs with my father. I want to grow up and grow old and keep the people I love safe. I wear briefs, although that's probably the least interesting question you've asked yet. The death penalty is sometimes needed, but often abused." He took a deep breath and hit the unlock button on his door, signaling that she should get out. "Nice chatting with you."

"You grew up with your dad? Me too. My mom passed away when I was a baby."

If she wanted to bond over that, she was barking up the wrong tree. "My mom isn't dead, she lived in another city with Jasper and our stepdad. Our parents were fucked and split their twin sons up before we'd even shared our first birthday."

Why had he shared that with her? He didn't talk about his childhood, ever. He didn't like reliving the worst years of his life. Maybe it was part of their connection. Maybe he was more likely to open up to her then he did with Pen and Baze. Shifters liked to think the universe controlled most things in life, including your relationships with other shifters. But as he'd said before, the universe could fuck off.

"Wow. That's awful." She unbuckled her seat belt and grabbed her small bag from the floorboard. "My mom didn't have a choice but to leave me with my father. I know she would have never wanted this for me, this life with him." Her voice changed when she spoke about her father. It was a tone he recognized, disgust. "He hates me because I'm nothing like him." She put her hand on the handle. "What about your dad? Did you two get along before he died?"

Before he died? Had he mentioned that Franklin was gone? He didn't think he had. Maybe Jasper had said something about it at lunch, or even last night when he was drunk.

"No." He didn't want to talk about Franklin with Axie. He didn't want any of his old life to touch her, dirty her relatively clean soul.

"So, you graduated this year? What's next? You have an empire that needs ruling or something?" Her voice was teasing, but the comment had raised his shackles.

What a fucking odd question. Why not ask if he had plans for college? Maybe Riley and Jasper were filling her in on everything about him. He needed to have a little talk with his pack. They needed to learn to keep their fucking mouths shut.

Either way, Jace wasn't sure how to answer her. Would she even understand if he told her that he was going to stay here in Haxton and take care of his family? Axie was human. Pack life would make no sense to her. Which was another reason he needed to put permanent distance between them.

He started to speak, fully prepared to make something up to get her out of the car. But then the front door opened and a man in a three-piece suit stepped out. Jace narrowed his eyes, his breath catching in his throat. He recognized that guy. Franklin had worked with him. He was a lawyer his father had used from time to time. He was one of those men who think they're at the top of the food chain when really they're so far at the bottom its comical.

"Who is that?" Jace pointed out Axie's window, making her turn her head back in the direction of her home. He studied her reaction, watching as she pulled her lower lip through her teeth and started to wring her hands in her lap.

"That's my father."

Motherfucker.

Miguel Contreau was a shifter, and he was an associate of Franklin's. He was a man who had ambition, who climbed the ladder like it was his fucking job. And his daughter was sitting here, asking question after probing question. Spouting facts that she shouldn't have even known. It didn't take long for everything to become crystal fucking clear to him.

"And you're daddy's little honey pot, right?"

"What?" Her eyes got bigger, her pulse thrumming in her throat. "What's that even supposed to mean?"

She knew exactly what he meant, and she was playing dumb. Playing a part, like she had been from the moment she'd come up to him last night at that stupid fucking party. This was why he didn't trust people, because everyone was out to get him. Out to screw with his happiness one way or another. He was hurt, but more than that he was pissed: at her, at himself, and at the shifter pacing inside of him.

Jace reached across her body, holding his breath so her scent wouldn't fill his senses and make him change his mind and claim her instead. "Get the fuck out."

"What? Why? I thought we were—"

"You thought you were getting all the information your lowlife father wanted. And we both damn well know it." He put his hands back on the steering wheel, taking shallow breaths, trying like hell to maintain his cool.

"Jace, no wait, you don't understand, please let me expl—"

"I said get out of my goddamn car, Axie." Jace stared straight ahead, afraid of the anger stirring in his veins. He wanted to scream. He wanted to fucking rage. But he couldn't seem to make himself do it. His shifter was in control at the moment, and his shifter would never let him hurt the girl still sitting next to him. "Are you stupid? I said get the fuck out."

She opened her mouth, like she had something to say. But he didn't want to hear it.

He whirled on her, letting some of his anger seep out, winding its way around them both with every word he spoke. "Your dad wanted you to get close to us, right? He wanted to find out what we had planned for the business now that Franklin was dead and gone. Or was it even more than that? Your old man pimping you out, sweetheart? Did he want one of us to fuck you? To fall for you?" *To claim her.*

Could that have been part of Miguel's plan? No. There was no way he'd possibly be able to predict Jace's reaction to his daughter. He shook his head, transferring some of his irritation over to himself. "I knew this would happen, I knew that someone would rise up and take my father's place. And you know what? As long as they stayed the hell away from me and the people I love, I wouldn't have given two shits. But your father invaded *my* space, and now I'm fucking pissed. So, unless you want me to lose my control and tear this car apart to get you out, I suggest you leave."

Axie stared at him for a few more moments, her eyes searching his like she was looking for something. She was gorgeous, absolutely beautiful, and even now when he was seething with rage, he wanted her. He wanted to grab her by the throat and pull her onto his lap. He wanted to sink inside her, he wanted to fuck her right here in his car with her father a few feet away. He wanted Miguel Contreau to watch while he quite literally took away his only child.

But he couldn't, he wouldn't. For so many damn reasons.

Jace broke their eye contact, choosing to stare straight ahead and slam the car into drive. She finally climbed out of the car, closing the door gently and turning her back to him as she made her way up to her house.

He kept his gaze on the road as he peeled out of her driveway.

He refused to look in his rearview mirror.

Axie Contreau and her conniving father had no place in his life.

Chapter Fourteen
Jace

Jace sent a group text when he was at a red light, and then sped the whole way home. His car was fast, expensive, and it hugged the curves on the winding mountain roads like a fucking dream. Usually he loved driving, turning the radio up and switching off his overactive brain. But today, Jace was too pissed to enjoy it.

He pulled into his driveway and squealed to a stop, throwing it in park and slamming his car door. Then slamming the front door for good measure. He'd done more slamming today than he had in his whole life.

"Hey, what's with all the teen angst?" Baze was on the couch, Pen's legs in his lap. He leaned back, his eyes on Jace as he crossed the shared space and poured himself a drink at his favorite vintage bar cart. "Isn't it a little early in the day for the hard stuff? What the fuck is up with you, kid?"

"I called a pack meeting."

Baze held up his phone, moving it from side to side. "Yeah, we got the summons, your highness."

"Bubs, what's going on? Is everything okay?" Pen pressed pause on whatever movie they'd been watching, then patted the space beside her. "Come tell me what's got you so irritated today."

Jace stared at Pen, taking in her kind smile and her concerned eyes. Of course she'd noticed that he'd been on edge all day. She worried over him, more than anyone in his life ever had. He wanted to tell her everything. He wanted to tell her that he'd met his mate, his forever. And that she was beautiful, sassy, and everything wild that he could never be. He wanted to tell them that she'd been sent by her father, and that everything he'd feared all these months was happening. That the haven he'd created for his pack had been breached and they were about to be thrown back into turmoil. He wanted Baze to fix all his problems, to take over and take the weight off his shoulders. He wanted Pen to hold him while he cried at the injustice of it all.

But the moment he'd taken one small step in their direction, the front door swung open and the rest of his pack started to file into the house. His hardened mask slipped smoothly into place and he took a sip of the whiskey in his hand. He was the beta. He was in charge of their safety. And no one could protect them from the dangers lurking in the shadows like him.

He couldn't be weak, ever.

"So, you can use nine-one-one texts but I can't?" Jasper plopped down on the couch, Maddi sitting between him and her mate Linc. Jasper absently rubbed a hand on her round stomach, his cosmic connection to her unborn daughter ever present. "Doesn't seem fair, man."

"Hadley needs a nap, so this better be quick." Corey handed the baby over to Riley, who went to stand off to the side, rocking her sweetly in his arms. "And by Hadley, I mean me."

Jace waited for Keller and Molly to filter in, and once everyone was seated he cleared his throat. "We have a problem."

"What's the name of the chicken that always thinks the sky is falling?" Jasper pulled out his phone. "I'll look it up."

"Chicken Little," Corey answered, reaching over and pushing Jasper's cell back into his lap. "We read that book to Hadley."

"Yeah, Chicken Little." Jasper pointed across the room at his twin. "You're like that, always thinking there's a problem. A danger lurking around every corner."

"Stop," Pen snapped, irritation in her tone, silencing Jasper. "You don't even know what he's about to tell us, let him talk."

Jace swallowed the rest of his drink, preparing himself to implode their world once again.

"Franklin was in charge of the Colorado underworld for as long as I can remember. He was ruthless, a killer. He climbed his way to the top and then did whatever necessary to make sure he stayed there. We all know the things he was capable of." Jace set his glass down, afraid that he'd end up shattering it in anger. "But Franklin didn't act alone. He had men who worked with him, men like him. His network was seemingly endless. And I knew that eventually, someone would rise to take his place. It's only natural, someone has to be the boss." He eyed Baze when he said this, letting him know silently that he was sorry for earlier. They communicated without words all the time, and Baze's small nod let Jace know he understood. "But I thought if I stayed out of it, if we kept to ourselves, they'd leave us alone."

"What you are saying? Did someone try to hurt you?" Pen sat up, putting her feet on the floor like she was fully prepared to go kick some shifter mob ass.

"No." Jace shook his head and Baze made her sit back down. "But there's been blood in the water since we killed Franklin and the sharks are starting to circle."

"You're being vague, and it's wearing me out." Dom leaned forward, making eye contact with Baze. "Make him talk."

Jace didn't need his alpha to force him to talk. Circumstance was making that choice for him. They were all in danger, again. "One of the men who worked with my father planted someone in our path. He was using them to get information on me." He looked at his twin. "On Jasper, on our plans now that Franklin is gone. He wanted to know if we were taking over, and he used his daughter to do it."

"Axie?" Jasper's forehead wrinkled, like he was having a hard time believing it. "Are you sure?"

He nodded. "I recognized her father today when I drove her home, and she all but admitted it. She was asking me tons of questions about Franklin, about my life. She knew things she shouldn't know."

"Who the hell is Axie?" Keller raised his hand.

"The girl from last night," Riley answered. "We met her at that party and it makes sense, she was super into us." He met Jace's eyes. "But that doesn't explain your reaction to—"

"Jasper trying to mount her?" Jace cut him off, redirecting what he'd been about to say. He wasn't ready to talk about his shifter's reaction to Axie. "Chivalry isn't dead for most of us."

Jasper rolled his eyes. "Come on, that's not fair. She was into us, dancing with us, making out with us. You said she freaked at the end, but I don't buy it. I'm pretty sure she would have been down for whatever we wanted."

"We? Us? Wait. Were you two planning to *share* her?" Corey glanced from Riley to Jasper. "Does that happen a lot? Or was this poor girl willing to go that far to get the information her father needed?"

Jasper's eyes got wide and Riley was looking anywhere but at Corey. Jace shook his head, sighing. "Now's not the time to get into what those two do with their dicks." He held up his hand when Linc opened his mouth to no doubt ask some further off-topic follow-up questions. "The fact is, Axie was planted. She was working for her father. If he's trying to take Franklin's place, then it stands that others are too."

Molly spoke up from her spot next to Keller, "So what does that mean for us? You and Jasper don't want anything to do with the things Franklin was involved in, right?"

"Of course not." Jace had never wanted to follow in his father's footsteps, whether he'd been groomed to do it from day one or not. "But it seems that no one believes that. Or else they wouldn't be poking their noses where they don't belong."

"Are we in danger here?" Dom was rubbing circles on Corey's back, his eyes on his daughter, who was resting peacefully in Riley's arms.

"If these men are thinking that Jasper and I want to rule in Franklin's absence, then yes, we're in danger. They'll try to take us out. You gain power in their world one of two ways. You're born into it, or you fucking fight to the death to earn it." Jace knew that his twin wasn't going to like the next thing that came out of his mouth. "Jasper, you're moving back to the house until I get this all sorted out."

"What? Why? I don't want shit to do with Franklin's business. I wasn't raised by him, no one even knows who the hell I am."

"You're the son who put a bullet in his heart." Jace's gaze went to the spot in his living room where his twin had killed their father. "They know that, and they won't overlook it. These men are calculated, and they'll take out every threat to their power they deem necessary. You took out a man like Franklin. You're a threat them."

"How exactly are you planning to sort this out?" Baze was on his feet now, no longer able to handle the submissive position. "More guns and violence?"

Jace knew Baze wasn't being a dick. He was worried about his pregnant mate and the rest of the pack. Any one of them could have died the last time there was an attack. They were beyond lucky they'd survived.

"I need to find the man most likely to win the race for power and convince him the throne is his to have." Jace understood the way these men worked. He'd been around their type his whole life. "Since Franklin died, I've basically been in hiding. I thought that would be the easiest way to show that I didn't want anything to do with his business. But I was wrong, it made people suspicious." He put his hands on his hips, hanging his head a bit. "I'm sorry. I've put you all in danger again and I apologize."

"Don't do that." Dom stood, crossing the room to put his hand on Jace's shoulder. "Just like last time, none of this is your fault."

Jace scoffed. "But exactly like last time, my father is the one that brought this all to our doorstep." He couldn't help but blame himself. If Jace had kept his distance, the way he'd been taught, nothing about Franklin or his life would have touched the people he'd grown to love.

Jasper shook his head. "He's our father, bro. And if it's your fault, then it's mine too."

"It's neither of your fault." Pen sent him a sad smile. "We're a pack. We're in everything together, always."

Jace would never be able to put into words how much his pack meant to him. For the first time in his life, he felt cared for. He felt like he was part of a family, like he was worth something. And he'd be damned if he let anyone get hurt. He'd fix this. He had no other choice.

"Jasper needs to be here, which should keep the focus off St. Leasing." Keller, Molly, Linc, and Maddi still lived on campus. Dom and Corey had bought a house in town, and Jasper and Riley were living in the apartment Baze and Linc used to share. If he could keep Jasper and Riley at his house until he had time to do some investigating, then the rest of the pack should be safe. All eyes would be pointed to his home in the mountains, which was a fortress. "Riley, I want you here too. I need all the focus here and diverted away from the girls."

Corey opened her mouth, her face indignant.

Jace cut her off before she could even begin to protest. "I don't want to hear any arguments about it either." He pointed at her, then at Maddi's swollen stomach. "Pregnant mates and mothers to infants are not allowed to get involved with this shifter mob bullshit, not again. And that's final."

They'd had to force the girls inside his safe room last time, and the stress of the whole situation had caused Corey to go into early labor. He wasn't about to put them in any more danger than they were already in. He knew his alpha and the rest of the guys in the pack would back him up. He was half tempted to send Baze and Pen away too. But that was a discussion for another time since no one else knew she was even pregnant.

Jasper got to his feet and tapped his fist on Riley's arm. "Come on, let's go pack a bag."

"Corey, take Hadley." Riley carefully placed the sleeping baby in her arms. "I'll come by to see her tomorrow."

"No you won't." Jace shrugged his shoulders, defeated. "I don't want connections made between us and them."

Riley scrunched up his freckled face. "I've been around Hadley every day of her life. The connection is already made."

"Look, I don't know what Axie has told her father. I don't know who else is after information. I don't even know what conclusions have been drawn." He glanced at Hadley, then back to Riley. "You're with Jasper all the time, you two are close. And if they think he's working with me to rule in Franklin's absence, they'll assume you're part of it too." Jace swallowed past the lump in his throat. "For all we know, they think the three of us are the next generation."

Chapter Fifteen
Axie

Axie winced as the sound of Jace peeling out of her driveway filled her ears. Gravel was flying and it was obvious to anyone watching that he was pissed. Fuck. She was so close to having something to tell her father, something to use to get him off her case. But no. Instead, she'd fallen all the way to square one. She doubted Jace would ever speak to her again after the things he'd said to her in that car. He'd looked like he'd wanted to kill her.

Except.

He also wanted her, she could tell. He was attracted to her, drawn to her, even though he didn't want to be. He couldn't help but look at her, watch her. Every time his gaze trailed over her body, he licked his lips. Did he even know he did that? Probably not because in those moments, it wasn't Jace who was in charge.

"Alexandra, what was that all about?" Her father crossed his arms over his chest, still standing on the porch. "Was that Jace Franklin? Why did he tear out of here like that?"

He left because he saw you, you fucking moron. "Uh, he had to go. Plans. I guess." She wanted to roll her eyes at herself. She was usually a much better liar than that. But Jace had shaken her to her core. She felt like she'd been thrown from a hot tub into an ice-cold swimming pool.

"Plans?" He narrowed his eyes, his hand striking out to grab her arm. "What did you do?"

"Why do you assume I did something?" She lifted her chin, refusing to let him know how much he was hurting her. "He brought me home, didn't he? I'm doing what you asked. I'm getting close to him."

He shook her roughly. "I told you to be careful. I told you that you needed to curb your attitude." He was snarling, getting closer and closer to her face with every word. "He cut out of here like he was angry." He tossed her to the ground, the concrete skinning her knees. "You can't fucking do anything right, can you?"

"What more do you want from me?" Axie got to her feet, unable to hold her anger and despair in check. "You whored me out to get intel on him, and I did it. I danced and I flirted, and I got an in." She threw her hands in the air. "He brought me home, and—"

"And then he threw you out of his car onto your ass." He sneered at her, disgust on his face. "You're worthless."

"We were talking, and then he saw *you*." She jabbed a finger in his chest, her control finally snapping. "He knew who you were, he knew what you were after. And he said you were nothing. That you didn't have the balls to take over for Franklin. He said you were nothing but a means to an end and you'd never—"

Her rant was cut off when her father backhanded her across her face. The pain radiated behind her eyes, making her drop to her already bloody knees. Her father had grabbed her, shaken her, yelled and screamed. But he'd never hit her before. And fuck, it hurt.

"I am more of a man than that stupid kid will ever be." He spit at the ground, narrowly missing her hand. "And you? I have no further use for you." Axie kept her eyes on his shoes, not wanting him to see her tears. As he turned and started to walk off in the direction of the garage he yelled, "Pack your shit and get out of my house, I'm done with your ineptitude."

She waited until she heard one of his many cars start up, wanting the sound of the expensive engine to drown out her cries. Axie never let her father see her tears. She'd decided from an early age that he didn't deserve them. They'd been close once, happy. But then her mother had passed away and everything had changed. He'd buried himself in work, and she lost her only remaining parent.

She wasn't upset that her father had kicked her out. She wasn't even worried that he'd stop his payment to UNLV. Now that she knew he was done with her and that he wouldn't come looking for her, he wouldn't drag her back here, she had nothing left to lose. Finally, she was free. The saltwater streaming down her face was from sheer frustration.

She'd fought with Jace. She'd fought with her father, and he'd hit her. She was sitting in front of her own home, bleeding all over the porch. And now she didn't know where she should go. When did this become her life?

She had friends, but they weren't real friends. A few of them had guesthouses she could crash in. But she couldn't show up there with her cheek swollen and bruised. Their parents would care, and they'd ask questions. Not everyone was raised by a monster, like her. Like Jace.

Jace.

Axie wanted to call him, wanted to try to explain. She wanted to ask him to come get her, to help her, to give her a safe place to lay her head at night. For some reason, he made her feel protected. But he'd made himself perfectly clear. He wanted nothing to do with her. And she couldn't blame him. She'd used him, or at the least, she'd planned to. Would she have gone through with it though? She wasn't sure.

She picked herself up off the ground, grabbing her purse from where it'd been thrown when her father backhanded her. Sighing, she let herself into the house, carefully making her way up the stairs. She'd shower, she'd change, and then pack a bag. Her father didn't take her car keys, because they were sitting on her nightstand. She could drive into town, hit up Moon Bar. Maybe she'd drown her sorrows for a bit, dull the pain in her face and her heart. Then she'd call a friend, find a place to crash for the night.

With a plan in place, she was already starting to feel a little better. Axie was great at compartmentalizing the terrible things that happened in her life. Which was the reason for the booze and the coke. It was easier to shove shit into a box in the back of her mind when she was high and dancing on tables.

Just what the doctor ordered for a wounded soul.

Chapter Sixteen
Jace

Jace was on his back porch, taking in the crisp Colorado evening air. Even in the summer, the temperature tended to drop at night. And since his home was surrounded on three sides by mountains, it was always a few degrees cooler than in town. He loved his house, his yard—his mountain. He felt at ease here, which was odd considering his brother had murdered his father in the living room.

"Hey, man, we're back." Riley stepped out the long sliding doors, taking a seat in one of his cushioned chairs. "We packed for at least a week."

Jace nodded, turning to sit across from him. "Good. How's Jasper? He still pissed that he has to be here?"

"Well, he's currently sitting in your sauna watching ESPN on the TV in there." Riley smiled. "So, I'd say he's clearly enjoying the lap of luxury."

"Nice." Jasper didn't like it when Jace bossed him around, and he didn't like feeling like he was a prison, like he was cooped up. It was the shifter in him, the shifter in all of them. But once Jasper calmed down, he'd remember that he had more freedom here in the mountains than he did in town. And he'd remember that Jace knew how to keep them safe.

Riley leaned forward, his forearms resting on his thighs. "Look, I understand why you don't want us around Axie, and I'll help you keep Jasper in line. He's in lust, not love, and that can easily be controlled." He gestured with his hands wide. "But what about you? What about you and Axie? We both know what your reaction to her meant. We know that she's your mate."

"Stop. We don't know for sure that she was meant to be mine." Jace shook his head, his molars grinding for a moment before he continued with his blatant lie. "And even if she was, Axie will be fine, I didn't touch her. Not once." Although he'd wanted to so fucking badly. "She'll go about her life, doing her father's bidding, marry one of his henchmen, and live a pretty predictable life."

"And what about you?"

Jace shrugged away his friend's concern. "I'm okay. I'm more than okay, I was never meant to have a soul mate, never—"

Riley cut him off, a scowl on his freckled face. "That's not true, man, everyone deserves to be happy, to be in love."

Riley was the most kindhearted out of the males in the pack. He cared deeply for everyone and everything. He wanted the world to be painted in shades of pink and everyone to get their happily ever after. Although he was a fuck boy like Jasper, he believed in love and fate and all that bullshit. And Jace admired that about him, he really did. Which was why he decided Riley deserved the truth from him for once.

"I know it's hard for the rest of you guys to understand when I say that I didn't grow up like you. But. It's true. I wasn't raised in a home filled with laughter and light. I didn't have two parents who adored me. I didn't get to play T-ball for the fun of it. I didn't get to have campouts with my friends, or drink, or date, or even party." He swallowed past the emotion in his throat. "I'm not bitter that I was the twin Franklin took. I'm happy that my brother had a good life. I'm glad that he grew up safe and loved." He smiled, looking into the house to see Pen walking up the stairs with a basket of clean laundry. "Becoming part of this pack, having Baze and Pen, you and Jasper… This life, it's more than I ever expected I'd get. So when I tell you I'm okay, please believe me."

Riley was quiet for a few minutes, the two of them sitting in companionable silence with the evening breeze blowing down from the mountains. Jace rarely put his emotions on the table like that. But he knew that if he wanted Riley to let go of his notion that Jace and Axie could ever be together, he needed to put all his cards on the table. Riley cared about his heart, and Jace truly wanted his friend to understand him, if only in one thing.

When Riley spoke again his tone was soft. "One day I hope that you realize how incredibly strong and special you are. How much you mean to all of us. How we'd fall apart without you. You think you're the lucky one, that this pack is more than you deserve. It's like you think you're tainted, like your darkness is a burden. But that's not true, bro." He got to his feet, his smile small and sad. "You protect us, and you watch over us. Our safety is your number one priority. You put us before yourself, always. We're the lucky ones, man. And if anyone in this pack should get a happily ever after, it's you."

Jace sat back, silent, as Riley stepped into the house. He'd love for all that to be true, for Riley's words to take root in his heart and spread out into his veins. Dragging happiness and light through his body, dispelling the hatred his father bred into him every damn day. But the scared and abused little boy inside him wouldn't allow it.

In his experience, people lied, and people hurt you.

Axie had proved that point only too well.

Chapter Seventeen
Axie

Moon Bar was packed tonight, and Axie was one glass of cheap champagne in when a large older man with salt-and-pepper hair came and sat next to her. Instantly, she wanted to move away from him, but then again, there were no other empty seats so maybe he was only there to order a drink.

"Hello there, sweetheart."

Well shit.

Axie fought the urge to let out an annoyed sigh because she wasn't in the mood. "Hello, sir." Maybe if she inadvertently pointed out that he was like twenty years older than her, he'd feel like a sleaze and leave her alone.

"Oh, sir? I like that, you can call me sir all night long."

Was this her life now? Was everything destined to go the opposite way of normal? As if her day couldn't possibly get worse, now a man old enough to be her father was hitting on her. Normally, she'd play along for a few minutes, then find an excuse to walk away. But tonight, she didn't have it in her. She'd had a shit day, and this douche was the cherry on top.

"You come here often, pretty girl?"

Yeah, she didn't have patience to deal with this. "Look, grandpa, you're too old to be talking to me." She tossed a twenty in the bartender's tip jar, dropping her voice to a whisper. "I'm not even old enough to be drinking in here." She downed what was left of her champagne, hopping off her barstool. "But something tells me you know that, and it makes your old shriveled dick hard."

The man's jaw dropped open. Was he really going to go for indignant right now?

"Who do you think you are talking to me like that?" His eyes searched the crowded space like he was looking for someone. "I should find the bouncer, have him kick your tight underaged ass out of here."

Yep. Indignant with a side of pedophile.

"No need, dickwad. I was leaving anyway." She grabbed the whiskey the bartender sat in front of him, throwing it back until it was empty. "Enjoy your night, but you know, stop hitting on girls young enough to be your daughter. It's gross." She sent him a tight smile and then turned on her heel, making her way through the throng of bodies and pushing the double doors open.

Axie let her head fall back, her arms out wide, deeply inhaling the crisp night air. Nothing made her feel better than handing men their asses like that. Between her interaction with that prick and the burst of alcohol now flowing through her veins, she felt like her night was really looking up.

She didn't need help. Nope. She could save herself. She could make herself feel better. Axie Contreau didn't need someone to pick her up when she was down. She was her own hype man.

Now, to find a place to sleep tonight. She pulled her cell out of her small clutch, walking in the direction of where she'd parked her car less than an hour ago. She pulled up her friends list, searching for her best option, using her thumb to scroll.

At first, she thought she'd tripped, which would have served her right for having her face on her cell while she was walking down the uneven sidewalk. But then, the next thing she knew, her feet left the ground entirely. One hand went over her mouth, one around her waist to drag her into the nearest dark alley.

Was this happening? Was she being mugged? In Haxton?

"Look, you don't need to hurt me. I have money, it's in my purse. I have cash and this necklace is stupid expensive. Take whatever you want, please don't—"

"Shut the fuck up bitch." Axie was backhanded for the second time in one damn day. This time though the man wasn't her father and he hit her lip instead of her cheek. She tasted blood, instantly. "I don't want your money." A leather gloved hand wrapped around the column of her throat. "I want to know about Jace Franklin."

Even though this wasn't the time for jokes, she couldn't seem to help her sarcastic reply. "Yeah, you and everyone else in fucking Colorado." He pulled her away from the wall, and then slammed her back into it. She probably had that coming. Axie promised whoever was in charge up there that if she lived through this, she'd try to be less sassy. "I don't know anything about him, I swear. You aren't the first person who's asked." She didn't need to tell the bad man that her father was the other person. Miguel Contreau had enemies.

"You're lying." His hold on her throat tightened. "I saw you with him, his pissant brother, and the redhead." He punched her in the side, making all the air leave her body in a harsh whoosh. "Tell me everything you know."

She gasped for a breath, unable to answer him right away. Which, of course, pissed him off and made him slam her against the rough brick again. "Fuck, I swear, I don't know anything. I met them all last night, and he, like, hates me."

The man smiled. She could see the motion through the black ski mask he was wearing. "I bet that's not true, a pretty thing like you." He leaned forward, his nose going to her hair to take a deep sniff that made her stomach turn.

Damnit. Could this fucking day get any worse? This was all her father's fault. He'd tried to pimp her out, then, with Jace sitting in the driveway, her idiot father had walked out of the house at the wrong moment. He'd disowned her and kicked her out as if it were her fault Jace knew who the asshole was. Man, her father was such a prick. If she lived through this, she might kill him herself.

"Maybe if I get you home, we have some fun and I take some pictures? I bet that would get a reaction out of those Franklin boys." His hand grabbed at her breast, the pain making her wince.

"You're wrong. They don't want anything to do with me."

"Yeah, well, we'll see, won't we?" One hand went to her mouth once again, which triggered her brain to realize that she could have been screaming her head off for the last three minutes. Hindsight was a motherfucker.

She fought, kicking and squirming as he started to drag her toward the entrance of the alley. For the first time she noticed a creepy matte black van parked along the curb. It looked suspicious as hell, and if she hadn't been so focused on her phone, maybe she would have seen it and been a little more on guard.

The man in black had her behind him as he peeked around the wall, making sure the coast was clear to no doubt take her to some gross basement with a dirty mattress on the concrete floor. She could picture it in her mind and she gagged behind his hand.

Without notice, his hold on her loosened as a group of women came out of Moon Bar laughing loudly.

Axie didn't waste time. She went limp and became straight dead weight like a toddler throwing a tantrum at the grocery store. She hit the ground and then jumped up and took off in a dead sprint toward her car. She pulled her key fob out of her pocket and hit the panic button. She refused to glance behind her. She had one thing on her brain and that was getting into her car and locking the doors.

The women who distracted the asshole for her were following her, trying to see if she was okay. But she was on autopilot. She couldn't answer, and she couldn't slow down. Axie jumped into her car, starting the engine, and her tires squealed as she pulled away from the curb.

She checked her rearview mirror, thankful when she didn't see the man or his creepy-ass kidnap van. Axie looked at the steering wheel, her eyes narrowing in disbelief. Her cell was still clutched in her shaky hand. Holy fuck. Why hadn't she used it as a weapon? Beamed him in the head with it?

That was it. As soon as she could, she was signing up for a self-defense class.

Axie pulled up her recent call list, dialing the one person she could think of calling and hoping like hell that he would pick up. And he did, after she called him on motherfucking repeat seven times.

"Stop calling me. I'm not supposed to talk to you, Jace told us what happened this afternoon and—"

"Riley, please god, don't hang up." She pulled in a deep breath, trying to keep her voice steady. "Please."

"What's wrong?"

"I was at Moon Bar, and when I left this guy grabbed me." She bit her lip for a moment wincing when her teeth touched the cut he'd given her, tears threatening to spill over. "He dragged me into the alley and he started questioning me about you, Jasper, and Jace."

"Oh my god, where are you now? I can come get you. I'm at Jace's but I can be in town in ten minutes. Are you safe? Call the police."

"No. No police." Police could end up causing Jace problems if he really had taken over in Franklin's absence. She didn't need to piss him off any more than she already had. "I need to talk to Jace. I need to warn him. I need to explain. If you could make him listen and—"

"Let me come get you."

"I'm already driving, I had to get away from there." She glanced around her, realizing that she'd been circling the streets of downtown Haxton the whole time she was waiting for Riley to get irritated enough to answer her call. "I hit my car alarm and he ran back into the alley, but I'm scared he'll come back. I can't go home because my dad kicked me out. Everything really fucking sucks right now, but if Jace could come meet me somewhere, then maybe I could explain and—"

"Axie, calm down. Take a few deep breaths, come on, in and out."

She did as he instructed, breathing with him.

"I'm going to send you an address, okay? I want you to come here to Jace's house."

"What? Why? He hates me. He'll be angry at you and he'll send me away." The look on Jace's face when he was yelling at her that afternoon…she'd never forget it.

"He'll be pissed, but he won't send you away. You were attacked, and this is the safest place for you right now."

Somehow she doubted that. But she didn't have anywhere else to go. She was on her own, and she was scared. As much as she hated to admit it, Riley's offer was the only one on the table. "Okay."

"But Axie? If you share this address with your father, with anyone… If you betray us, there will be consequences."

"I won't, I swear."

She'd asked the universe if her day could possibly get any worse, and it looked like she was about to find out.

Chapter Eighteen
Jace

The sun had set hours ago and Jace was sitting in his office, staring at all his monitors. Checking security cameras had become a compulsion of his. He liked seeing that everyone he cared for was safe. It brought him such a sense of peace, and seemed to calm his restless mind and his constantly pacing shifter.

Riley and Jasper were here, and the alarms were all set. The rest of his pack had state-of-the-art alarms too. He'd paid for everyone to be set up with the best of the best. And that was when he'd secretly installed the rest of the cameras around their homes.

It wasn't as invasive as it sounded. The feeds only showed him the outsides of their houses, the street, the doors, and windows. He needed to be sure that no one could sneak up on them.

He clicked through with his mouse, checking the perimeter of his compound one more time before bed. He paused, his eyes narrowing as he spotted a car coming up his long driveway. Was someone lost? Or were they about to be attacked? Was it already starting?

His heart started to pound, his jaw clenching and unclenching as he saw the car stop and punch in the combination at his gate. No one had that combination, no one but his pack. And he changed it every two to three days to be sure that his home stayed secure.

Which meant they'd been compromised.

He stood, his chair ramming into the wall behind him as he made his way out of his office and down the short hallway to the living room.

Jasper and Baze were on the couch, a giant bowl of popcorn between them. He could hear Pen and Riley talking in the kitchen.

"There's someone here, they knew the gate code and they're coming up the driveway." He grabbed the gun from the back of his pants, switching off the safety.

"Whoa, bubs, what's going on?" Pen came in from the kitchen, a tray of drinks in her hand. "Baze?"

"I don't know, he said someone is here." Baze got to his feet, taking the tray from Pen and setting it on the coffee table as he pushed her behind him.

"Oh, uh, wait. It's not what you—"

There was a knock at the door cutting off whatever Riley had been about to say. Jace held his hand up, making sure that everyone knew to be quiet. He made his way to the entryway, fully prepared to do whatever it took to make sure his pack stayed safe. He opened the reinforced peephole slide, his gun drawn and ready.

"What in the actual fuck?" Jace whirled around, his gaze moving between Riley and Jasper. "Why is Axie on my goddamn front porch? How did she get this address? The gate code? What the hell were the two of you thinking?"

Jasper held his hands in the air, like he was surrendering. "It wasn't me, bro, I swear."

Jace's glare zeroed in on Riley. "You?"

Riley nodded as he glanced to the door when she knocked again. "She called me a few minutes ago. She was attacked outside of Moon Bar. Someone was questioning her about us." He shrugged. "She wouldn't let me come get her, and her father kicked her out." He moved past Jace, his palm closing around the front door handle. "You can be pissed at me later, but right now, we need to find out who the hell else is asking questions about us."

Riley had a point, which was the only reason Jace stepped back and let him open the door. He'd interrogate Axie, and then send her packing. Her father kicked her out. Good. She got what was coming… His thoughts died a quick death when he saw her standing on his porch, her shirt ripped, her body shaking and bleeding.

His shifter eyes started assessing her injuries, cataloguing the scent on her skin, trying to figure out what to do first. Kill the person responsible or hide Axie away somewhere safe that no one else could get to her.

"Oh my god, Axie." While Jace had been trying to wrap his brain around what to do, Riley leapt outside and was about to pull her into his arms.

"Don't touch her," Jace growled, speaking through clenched teeth. His body was vibrating, his shifter begging to be let out. He wanted to follow the scent still clinging to her skin, he wanted to find who hurt her and rip him apart. He wanted to tear that man's still-beating heart from his chest.

But he also wanted to pick her up and lick all her wounds clean.

"Dude, look at her, she needs our help." Riley reached for her again. "You can kick her out after she's had a chan—"

"Step away from her or I'll kill you." Jace took a deep breath, trying like hell to regain even an ounce of control over the chaos coursing through his body.

Riley held his hands up, backing away, finally realizing what Jace was telling him.

Once Riley was back in the house, Jace stepped onto the porch and pulled the door shut behind him.

"Do you need a doctor?" he spoke softly, trying like hell to keep from snarling.

Axie shook her head, her arms wrapped around her still-shaking body.

"Are you going to go into shock?"

She shook her head again.

"I'm going to pick you up now."

"W-Why?" Her teeth started to chatter.

Valid question since he'd been mean to her for the last twenty-four hours. He could lie, he could back away and let her walk. But in the end, he was honest. "Because my urge to help you is stronger than my urge to fight at the moment."

She swayed on her feet, nodding her acceptance.

Cautiously, Jace stepped into her space, bending down a bit so he could cradle her in his arms. He held her close against his chest, thankful when Riley opened the front door for him to carry her through. Jace kicked the door closed, and walked past Riley, his brother, his alpha, and Pen. He knew they had a million questions, and he could hear some of them as he made his way up the stairs, grateful when Riley answered them as vaguely as possible.

"Who was that girl?"

"That's Axie."

"She needs our help. I should go up there."

"No. Leave them be. He's not in control right now."

"What do you mean? Jace is always in control."

"Not when it comes to Axie."

"But he was acting like—"

"I'm sure he'll explain it all when he's ready."

Jace shut the guest room door behind him, pausing to throw the lock into place. He turned on the light in the adjoining bathroom, setting Axie on the sink, his hand on her face tilting it toward the light to assess the damage.

"I'm sure it's not as bad as it looks."

He ignored her, because she was wrong, and because his wolf was begging to be let out to hunt down the man responsible.

Her nose was bleeding, she had a bruise on her cheek, and her lip was split open. There was a handprint around her throat, and she winced when Jace's fingers trailed across the battered skin. He took a small step back, taking the hem of her shirt and pulling it up over her head. She didn't fight him. Instead she watched him gently study her injuries while tears spilled down her cheeks. Jace lightly prodded her ribs, making sure that none of them were broken. He dropped down to the ground, his thumbs grazing her skinned knees.

"Well, what's the verdict? Am I going to live long enough for you to get a chance to kill me?" Axie laughed quietly, like she was trying to make light of a dark situation.

Jace stood, his chest heaving with every breath. He still wasn't in full control, and staring at the beautiful girl crying silently in front of him made him wonder if he ever would be again.

"Who did this to you?" He hardly recognized his own voice, the barely contained rage vibrating in his tone.

"I, uh, I don't know."

Jace took a washcloth out of the cabinet behind him, running it under hot water. "What did he say?" Axie sucked in a sharp breath when he started to clean up the cuts on her face. "Is there anything you remember?"

"He, um, he wanted to know about you. He mentioned Jasper and Riley too." Her chin dropped to her chest, seeming to realize for the first time that he'd taken off her top. "He said he saw me with you guys and when I tried to tell him that we weren't close, that I didn't know anything, he said he was going to take me home, take some pictures to send to you."

Jace's growl was deep and rumbling, his hands fisted at his sides.

"He said if we had some fun, that he bet it would get a reaction out of you guys." Axie was speaking quietly, like she was almost afraid of the sounds coming from low in his throat.

"Did he? Did he, fuck, did he…" Jace was having a hard time getting his words to form properly. He was terrified of her answer, terrified of what his reaction would be. He'd kill, and he'd tear through anyone who got in his way.

"No." Axie shook her head, her hands coming to rest on his shoulders. "A group of people walked by the alley and it distracted him. I ran, and then hit the panic alarm on my car key."

Jace hated that she'd been hurt because of him. One more mark against his soul. One more person who suffered because of their connection to him. Would it ever fucking end?

He had the urge to heal her. He wanted to make every ache feel better. Or maybe, his wolf did. Either way Jace dipped down, placing a kiss on each scrape on her knees, unable to help himself. He stood, placing his lips on her ribs, her neck, her jaw. Then he pulled back, his eyes meeting hers, the heat building between them undeniable.

"I'm sorry this happened to you, Axie."

She shrugged, a small smile on her beautiful and battered face. "You forgot one." She tapped her swollen bottom lip, her finger next to the long clean cut.

He smirked, despite himself. How could she laugh and make jokes at a time like this? But if she could manage a smile, then he could manage one small kiss.

"Try not to move, okay?" Her forehead wrinkled like she was confused by his direction. "I'm not in control right now, none of this is me. It's all him, it's all my shifter. And if you move, or try to take things further, he'll react. Do you understand?"

Axie knew he was a shifter. She'd been raised by one. Which made him wonder if she felt their connection. Did she know what he was to her?

He leaned in, softly kissing her lips. He was proud of himself, and proud of his wolf. He'd cleaned her up, and he'd stayed calmer than he ever thought possible.

That was until he inhaled deeply, letting his guard down, and smelled another male on the girl that belonged only to him. *Mine.* He grabbed her hips, pulling her core flush against his body, making her gasp in surprise. He used the opening to take the kiss deeper, devouring her, forgetting all about her split lip. She wrapped her legs around his waist, her fingers tangling in his hair, showing him that she had forgotten her injuries for the moment as well.

Nothing had ever felt like this. Nothing could be better than having Axie in his arms, his lips moving with hers. The soft whimpers escaping her throat, the growls echoing in his. This was primal. This was instinct. This was what he was made for, claiming what was his.

Wait.

No.

She wasn't his.

She'd lied to him. She'd used him.

The universe made a mistake.

A big fucking mistake.

Jace put his palms on her shoulders, shoving her back, breaking their kiss. They were both breathing hard, their chests heaving. He couldn't look at her, he couldn't meet her beautiful green eyes, so instead he turned and threw a solid punch into the sheet rock behind him, the pain in his hand distracting him from the pain in his soul.

He kept his back to her as he spoke, "You can't leave now that you know where I live, not that your weasel of a father would let you come home anyway." He opened the bathroom door, still refusing to look at her again. He was afraid that if he did, his fragile resolve would crumble. "You can sleep in this room until we figure out what to do with you."

With those words, he walked out, shutting the door firmly behind him.

Chapter Nineteen
Axie

Axie opened her eyes, stretching her arms over her head, momentarily confused as to where she was, and asked herself what happened last night. Who had she hooked up with? She didn't recognize the sheets wrapped around her body or the king bed she was lying in. She winced as she darted her tongue out to lick her dry lips. Her lip was split. What... Oh.

Everything came flooding back into her brain: Moon Bar, the gross old man, the attack in the alley. She'd called Riley and he'd told her to come here. To Jace's house.

Jace.

She could picture his face last night when he opened the door and saw her. His jaw grinding, his fists clenched. At first she thought he was going to rage, to hit her. But then she realized that he was reacting to the way she looked, to the blood on her face and the fear she had to have been wearing. It was their connection. It was his shifter. He wouldn't let Riley touch her, and Jace carried her up the stairs, into this room. He had taken care of her. He'd checked her injuries. He cleaned her up and kissed every bruise, every cut. He'd softened to her. They'd shared a moment, a small space in time where he wasn't trying to push her away.

But then he had. Literally. He shoved her back, then he'd punched a hole in the wall.

Axie sat up in bed, leaning forward to peek into the adjoining bathroom. Yep. There was a fist-size hole in the sheetrock. He'd been pissed that he let her in, that he'd kissed her.

Jace had kissed her. Had touched her.

If he was meant to be hers, if she was made to be his… Jace had started the bonding process. He'd set the rest of their lives into motion with that one sweet moment.

She knew that their initial connection had been something special. She'd never chased after anyone the way she had him. Her body sought out his, wanting to be near him in a way that she'd never experienced before. And last night, when she'd been lying in bed, alone and missing him, everything started to click in her mind. The words he'd used in the bathroom, the way he'd healed her, his reaction to Jasper's teeth on her flesh. Maybe it all meant something more. Or maybe she was reaching, seeing things that weren't there.

Axie fell back against the soft pillows, her breath hitching when the sudden movement hurt her ribs.

She rested her forearm over her eyes, wishing she'd shut the heavy rose gold curtains before she'd climbed into Jace's massive guest bed. The sun was bright and her head was starting to pound. She needed coffee and pain medicine. Her father had hit her, some random asshole had kicked her around, and then Jace had pulled her close only to push her away. All in all, not a great day.

"Hey, sleeping beauty, you ready to join the world?"

She sat up, smiling when she saw Riley leaning against the doorframe. "If it isn't my favorite redhead."

"I might be a dead redhead by the time this day is over." He stepped into the room and sat on the edge of her bed. "I haven't seen Jace yet this morning, but I'm guessing he's pretty fucking pissed that I let you come here last night."

She crawled down the mattress, curling up beside her newest friend. "I appreciate you putting your neck on the line for me. I really didn't have anywhere to go."

"Your dad kicked you out?"

"Yeah." She rested her head on his shoulder. "He saw Jace get mad at me, and he pretty much disowned me for fucking that up."

"So you *were* working for your dad? Gathering information? That's why you came up to the three of us at the party, why you wanted to hang with Jasper and me? It was all because your father wanted you to, and you were fully prepared to sell us out?"

Well fuck, when he put it like that she felt like she was two inches tall. "Yes, and no." She sat up crossing her legs in front of her so she could look him in the eyes when she owned up to all her truths.

"My father came to me before I left for the party. He told me Jace would be there, he told me he wanted information on him. He wanted to know if Jace was taking Franklin's place." She moved her hair over one shoulder, a nervous habit. "My father threatened to pull the funds he sent to UNLV, said if I didn't help he'd cut me off."

"You sold us out for money?"

"No." She shook her head. "I didn't sell you out. I didn't even plan on it. I was going to get him enough information to keep him busy, buy myself some time. I thought I could make friends with you guys, feed him some dumb bullshit, and then leave early for school." She reached for Riley's hands, pleading with him to understand. "My father is awful, and he's controlling. I've been waiting, biding my time, counting down the days until I'd be free. I knew if I refused him, he'd do exactly what he did. And if I ran, he'd drag me back and do this," she motioned to her body, "to me. I didn't know you, any of you. And I didn't expect, well, I didn't expect Jace."

It felt right letting Riley in, telling him that Jace affected her.

"Jace doesn't let people in easily, and you broke his trust before he could even give it to you."

She took a deep breath, falling back into the pile of pillows again. "You're telling me that I'm shit out of luck and he'll never be able to stand the sight of me." What would she do if that were the case? Was that even possible? For him to hate her for eternity. It couldn't be, not if she was right about what their connection meant. "Because I would deserve that, I was a real brat."

Riley chuckled, standing and then grabbing her hands to pull her back to sitting. "You two are a lot more alike than either of you realizes." He got off the bed and crossed the room, opening a closet that appeared to have clothes hanging from the metal rods. "Jace, the guy who can't stand the sight of you, went and got your bags out of your car." He turned to face her, a tight smile on his face. "You need to get dressed. We're having a pack meeting and you need to tell us everything you know about your father and about the man who attacked you."

A pack meeting?

"You guys live in a pack? I didn't think those existed anymore." Sure, she'd read books, picked up information here and there from eavesdropping on her father's conversations. But from everything she'd been taught, packs were a thing of the past. Like hand washing clothes and churning butter.

"We do, and they do, sort of." He headed toward the door. "And if you know what's good for you, you'll speak when spoken to and otherwise keep that pretty mouth of yours shut."

"Why?" She crawled off the bed, scrambling after Riley with the knowledge she needed to survive another day in Jace's house. "Is that a pack thing? Is it because I'm an outsider?"

He paused, his hand on the heavy brass doorknob. "Well, you *are* an outsider, Axie. But you need to watch what you say because I'm almost positive that Jace is on a hair trigger when it comes to you. And one wrong move could push him over the edge."

"And then he'll snap and kill me?" She voice was small, more than a little wary.

Riley shrugged casually. "Kill you or claim you, never can tell with him."

And those were his parting words.

Axie stared at the door, letting that information settle into her brain until her cell phone dinged on the nightstand beside her. Someone had plugged it into a charger that didn't belong to her. Jace. He'd come in here last night after she'd fallen asleep, unpacked her suitcase, and charged her phone. He'd probably bugged the stupid thing. It didn't matter. She didn't have anything left to hide from him.

Jace: Get dressed.

Oh. He'd added his number as well. Which meant he'd easily gotten past her passcode, and had no doubt gone through the thing with a fine-toothed comb. She bet he didn't appreciate some of those naughtier text messages she had with a couple guys from... Son of a bitch. Nosy bastard had deleted every single one of her text chains.

Riley's words floated through her brain: *kill you or claim you.* Jace certainly was a jealous little wolf, wasn't he?

Axie: Yes, your highness.

Jace: My whole pack is coming. You need to watch your mouth. What happened between us last night is no one's business. Do you understand?

Axie: No worries, Riley already warned me.

Jace: When?

Axie: Uh, like, three minutes ago when he came in here to wake me up.

Jace: Riley has no business being in your room. Keep the door locked from now on.

Was he really that jealous, or was he that utterly controlling of his home and the people who stayed here? Either way, she wasn't in a position to argue with him. And possessive didn't bother her all that much anyway. She'd grown up that way. She'd learned a long time ago that it was simply easier to say *yes sir* and then do whatever she wanted when backs were turned.

Axie: Whatever.

Chapter Twenty
Jace

Jace hadn't slept last night. He was going on twenty-four hours wide awake. After he'd left Axie in her room, he'd gone down to his office and contacted Mathias. He was an excellent hacker, and he'd proved himself more than loyal when they'd faced Franklin a few months ago. Mathias was back in Spain with his pack, but the help Jace needed didn't require Mathias's physical presence.

Once he had their plan ironed out, he'd gone out front and searched Axie's car. He needed to make sure that there wasn't a tracker on it. He disabled the GPS and carried her bags into the house. She was sound asleep in his guest room, one toned leg on top of the covers and one underneath. He reached a hand out, wanting more than anything to touch her again. But she'd rolled over, her shirt riding up and exposing her bruised ribs. Which reminded him of their time in the bathroom, and the reason he'd shoved her away.

He'd dismantled her cell, making sure it couldn't be traced and that the only bug in there was the one he placed. By that time it was close to sunrise, but he couldn't make himself leave the room. Instead he'd unpacked her bags and then sat in the chair across from her bed, watching her while she slept. He was drawn to her, intrigued by her.

His shifter wanted to sink inside her body, bite her flesh and make her scream their name. When the temptation got too great, he fled the room and headed to the basement gym. By the time he was done with his workout, the rest of the house was starting to wake.

He sent out another group text to the pack, and then locked himself in his office. He didn't want to see the question in Pen's eyes, or the concern in Baze's. He didn't want to hear Riley tell him that he deserved to be happy, and he didn't want to listen to his twin talk about how perfect Axie's ass was.

He hid from them all, watching the monitors as the rest of the pack arrived at the house, one by one. When he knew they were all gathered in the living room, he texted Axie to get dressed.

And now there was nothing left to do but go out there and face her. Face everyone. Would they be able to tell? Would they see the desire in his eyes? The slight shake in his hands? Fuck, he hoped not.

He left his office, turning the corner into the great room, deciding that getting right to business would be the best course of action. "Thank you all for coming on short notice."

"Why does it sound like you're addressing a fucking boardroom?" Linc dropped his head back on the couch, his hands scrubbing down his blond stubble. "And why are we here so damn early, beta?"

"Because this couldn't wait." And because he'd been up for a whole day and he knew he'd crash at some point. "Does anyone else have any smart-ass comments, or can I get started?"

"I do." Dom raised his hand. "You look like hammered dog shit. When's the last time you slept?"

Jace's gaze darted to Axie. "That's not really relevant to why you're here." She was sitting between Jasper and Riley, which straight pissed him off. She looked good, really fucking good. She'd managed to cover most of her bruises with makeup and her dark hair was full and wild. She was wearing ripped jeans and a loose-fitting army green tank top, her feet were bare, and he could smell her perfume from across the fucking room.

"Axie was attacked last night outside of Moon Bar by a man who was asking questions about me, Jasper, and Riley." He sighed, dragging his gaze back to the rest of the room. "A man she didn't recognize, which proves my point. The sharks are circling."

"So this is the famous Axie?" Baze sat forward, peering around Pen to take a good hard look at her. He was trying to intimidate her, alpha style. Which Jace sort of appreciated, because it meant that Baze wasn't forgetting her betrayal.

"Yep. I'm Axie." She waved to the room, a cheesy smile on her face. "I know that most of you probably hate me, and I don't blame you, but—"

"What happened to you keeping your pretty mouth shut?" Riley cut her off, a what-the-fuck look on his face.

Jasper snorted, crossing his arms over his chest. "More like sexy mouth."

"Enough," Jace snapped out. He tolerated Riley talking to Axie like that, but not Jasper. His twin had touched her, he'd had his teeth on her flesh, and he'd already stepped way over the line when it came to their current fucked-up situation.

Axie licked her lips, drawing all three unbonded males' attention. "I want everyone to know that I'm sorry, and that I would have never given my father any information that could have gotten any of you hurt." She shrugged her small shoulders, making Jace want to sink to his knees and mark her neck. "I was going to get bare minimum bullshit to buy myself enough time to get out of Colorado. But that was before…" She trailed off, her eyes darting briefly to Jace.

Riley had warned her to keep quiet, and it seemed that she was at least going to keep part of that promise. Jace wasn't ready to examine his connection to her, and he sure as fuck wasn't ready to have the rest of his pack doing it either.

"Before what?" Keller wrinkled his forehead, his gaze shooting around the room. "Why does it feel like we're all missing something?"

"Before we all became friends." Riley put his hand on the back of Axie's chair, the gesture familiar and irritating as hell to Jace's wolf. "Getting the shit kicked out of you by bad guys tends to bring people together, right, Ax?"

Ax. Now Riley was giving her a nickname? Fucking perfect. Jace wanted to fly across the room and murder his friend. Or, at the very least, rip off his arm and pull out his tongue.

"Okay, so tell us what you know about your father, and the guy who jumped you last night." Baze got to his feet, never one to stay seated for too long. The alpha in him demanded he stand while addressing his pack.

"Well, my father is an attorney. He defends criminals. He wasn't always this power hungry though. When I was younger, he was an average lawyer, home by six o'clock and smiling at the dinner table. After my mother died, he buried himself in work. The older I got, the more I noticed how wrong things had become. Upgraded mansion.

The most expensive cars. There were always extra men coming in and out of our house. Increased security, cameras, and drivers."

She cleared her throat, her chin lifting like she was infusing strength into her spine. "I don't even know the man he's become. We aren't close. We rarely speak. When he demanded I get close to Jace, I pretty much blew him off. But he got real angry and aggressive. He threatened to keep me here like a prisoner, to pull the funds he'd sent to Nevada for me to go to school. So, I figured I could feed him insignificant little facts until it was time for me to move out."

"He asked you to get close to Jace? Or Jasper and Riley too?" Dom was perched on the edge of the couch, like he was ready to scoop up all the information she was spilling. He was no doubt worried about Riley, who was like a son to him.

"Jace." She looked across the room at him again, her pulse visible in her enticing throat. "He, uh, he wanted me to lure in Jace. But I met Jasper first and I figured an in was an in, right? I didn't really care who gave me the tea to spill. And Jasper and Riley were much more open to spending time with me than Jace."

"Apparently my survival instincts are better than theirs." Jace sent his twin and best friend a sarcastic smile.

"No doubt." Jasper put his hands behind his head. "I'd have let Axie slit my throat as long as she was riding my—"

"Stop fucking talking." Jace ground out his words through clenched teeth. His heart was starting to hammer inside his chest so hard that it was painful. His shifter was getting agitated.

"Let me get this straight: Your father tried to pimp you out to Jace, but he didn't take the bait." Maddi rubbed a hand on her rounded stomach. "Tweedle Dee and Tweedle Dumb over there were super into you though, so you figured you'd get the information from them?" Axie nodded so Maddi kept going. "Okay, then what pissed off your father? Seems to me like you were getting what he wanted."

"Jace drove me home yesterday, and he saw my father come out of the house." She licked her pouty lips again and Jace's dick got ridiculously hard. Fucking perfect. "Jace got pissed, peeled out of my driveway, and my dad slapped me around, and then kicked me out."

"He did what?" Jace's attention moved from her mouth to her eyes. "He hit you?"

Axie pointed to the barely noticeable bruise under her left eye. "Yeah, this one is him, and the skinned knees." She waved her hand around the rest of her body. "Everything else is the asshole who attacked me outside Moon Bar."

Well, now he needed to murder two people who hurt the girl that belon... Axie.

Baze was standing beside him, his hands on his hips. "Why did you get mad at her? When you saw her dad, I mean."

"Axie was asking me all these stupid personal questions, and when I recognized her father, I put two and two together." He winced so slightly that only Baze caught it. "I lost my shit. I may have shoved her out of the car before I threw gravel all over the place."

"Sounds about right." Linc nodded, like everything made perfect sense to him.

Keller sighed, sounding as weary as Jace felt. "And the guy from Moon Bar?"

"He pulled me into an alley, kicked my ass, and didn't believe me when I told him that I didn't know anything about Jace, Jasper, or Riley." Axie rubbed at her temples, her eyes closing as she continued. "I don't remember what he looked like. He was wearing a ski mask. He kept his voice quiet, like he was whispering the whole time. I got away as soon as I could, which is when I called Riley and he gave me the address to the house."

Oh that's right, the fact that Axie was in his home, wreaking havoc on his resolve was all Riley's fault.

"A general housekeeping note for the whole damn pack. Don't give out this fucking address. Ever." Jace mirrored Baze's power stance, glaring at Riley.

"She was sobbing on the phone, what else was I supposed to do?" Riley threw his hand in the air, exasperated.

Riley's kind heart was going to get them all into trouble one day, there was no doubt in Jace's mind. But he couldn't seem to gather enough anger at the moment to keep lecturing him about it. His shifter liked that Axie was here in his space, safe and close. But his shifter was a dumbass.

"What's the plan, beta?" Linc asked the question, but everyone in his pack turned their attention to him to hear the answer.

"I contacted Mathias." Jace ignored Linc's obvious eye roll at the mention of Maddi's old friend. "He's getting me all Franklin's dossiers. They're password protected and encrypted, but he doesn't think it'll be hard to get past all his safeguards. And with those, I'll start compiling a list. I'll figure out who's the lead in this stupid race for power, and I'll ask for a meeting."

He'd ask for a meeting, and he'd try to convince them that as long as they left him and his pack alone, he wouldn't stand in their way. He hoped that would work because he hadn't come up with a Plan B. He was easily distracted by Axie, and by the fact that she kept garnering all kinds of male attention, good and bad.

"What do you need from us?" Corey handed Hadley to Riley, coming to stand in front of him. "Tell us what we can do to help."

He smiled when she wrapped her arms around his waist, hugging him briefly. "Stay safe, stay together. Don't go anywhere alone. Don't go out at night. Lay low until I have all this figured out."

"We." Jasper spoke up, "Until we have this figured out. Me, Jace, and Riley." He shook his head. "You're not alone, bro, never again."

All the females in the room melted at Jasper's sweet words, which made the jackass preen like a peacock. Jace's twin was irritating, cocky, and constantly distracted. But Jace couldn't deny that his brother had his back. And with the way things were going, it was going to take more than only his brain to figure this out. Especially since a big portion of his mind was preoccupied with the gorgeous dark-haired girl currently cooing at the happy baby in Riley's lap.

Chapter Twenty-One
Axie

After the pack meeting, Axie escaped to her room upstairs. She knew that no one trusted her, and she didn't want to push the issue by trying to hang out with them like they were friends. Anyway, she felt tired. Her body was trying to heal from all the shit that it'd been put through the day before.

She climbed into the large bed with the fluffy white blanket, burying her face in her hands. She was alone now, so she could cry. Axie didn't like letting other people see her tears, see her weaknesses. In her experience, if people knew how to hurt you, they would. No one in the house cared for her, except maybe Riley. She wasn't worried about being interrupted, so she let sobs wrack her body. She took deep breaths, crying into one of her pillows. Her shoulders were shaking, her body rocking back and forth. She let it out, all of it. Everything that had happened with her father since her mother died, the terror of being attacked, and Jace's constant rejection.

"Axie."

She stopped breathing, slowly looking up to see Jace standing in the doorway. Tears were still silently falling down her face, but at least she was able to hold in her hiccups.

"You're crying."

She nodded. "I've had a really shitty couple of days."

She watched him watch her. Sometimes, he stood so still, like he was prepared to think about every move before he made it. This was one of those times. She knew he was arguing with himself: a debate was going on behind those dark eyes. He wanted to walk away from her, but he wanted to come closer too. His human brain versus his shifter heart: fighting against and for the inevitable.

"I think we could both use some rest."

She nodded again.

Jace stepped into her room, his shifter heart winning this one. He closed and locked the door behind him, sending her a pointed look. He'd told her to keep her bedroom door locked, and she hadn't. He walked over to the large floor-to-ceiling windows, pulling the curtains closed, blanketing them in darkness. He kept his eyes on hers as he pulled his shirt over the back of his head before laying it neatly on an upholstered chair by the bed.

Her skin felt instantly heated, like she was going to catch fire from the inside out. She'd never seen anyone as utterly mesmerizing as Jace Franklin. His chest was defined, his waist trim, the V leading down into his slacks was making her drool. His arms, his hands: everything about him was enticing.

"Don't try to touch me." Jace shook his head slightly, his voice soft as he climbed into bed beside her. "Lie down, and face the wall."

Axie couldn't explain why she listened to him when he commanded her like that. But she did. Without hesitation she lay down, turning onto her side, adjusting the pillow under her head. She was holding her breath again in anticipation of what Jace would do next, what he'd say. She was hungry for every tiny morsel of communication, and for his touch. She'd take him any way she could get him, even if he'd only end up pushing her away again in the end.

Jace's arm slipped around her waist, his chest pressed to her back. He pulled her tighter against him, burying his face in her neck, inhaling deeply.

"Sleep, Axie." His lips moved against her skin, sending chills down her spine.

Instead of being nervous or on edge that he was here and holding her, she instantly calmed. Her heart slowed, her breathing evened out, her tears dried up. It didn't make any sense, but having Jace like this, it made everything seem right in the world.

***

Axie woke, feeling a loss. She knew their moment was over, she knew that he'd push her away once again. She turned, expecting to find the bed empty and Jace long gone. But he was still there, sitting on the edge, his head in his hands.

"You hungry?"

His tone wasn't soft anymore: it was back to hard and cold. She'd been right. He was about to wedge distance between them. He was going to ignore the fact that they'd slept the day away, wrapped in each other's arms.

"Why don't we stay in bed?" What she really meant was, stay here in the dark where he wasn't so fucking mean to her, where he wasn't so distant.

"I shouldn't have come up here, I shouldn't have—"

"Showed me kindness? Held me? Let me in, even a little bit?" She sat up, pulling her hair over her shoulder. "I know what's coming Jace, I know that you're about ten seconds away from punishing us." She threw her hands in the air, her patience running out with his hot and cold. Her already frayed nerves were close to snapping. "Why am I even here? Why didn't you kick me out? Put me in the basement? Or in a remote creepy cabin in the woods? What am I in doing in your home, in this guest room?"

Did he enjoying torturing himself and hurting her?

"You're here for one reason and one reason only." He stood, keeping his back to her as he headed to the door. "Because I keep my enemies real fucking close."

Axie rose up on the knees, pleading, "I'm not your enemy, Jace, I've been nothing but honest with you."

"Sure, Axie, you've been nothing but honest with me." He scoffed, finally turning to face her. "From the moment, I caught you in a goddamn lie."

She licked her lips, knowing that he would take notice. "You and I, we aren't so different. I know what it's like to grow up with an egotistical asshole for a father."

He threw his head back, a humorless laugh tearing through his throat. "*Egotistical?* You think my father was an asshole?" He pointed at himself. "My father was evil incarnate. He was abusive and violent and cold. You don't know the first thing about how I grew up."

"Maybe not, but I know what it feels like to want to get away." She crawled off the bed, coming to stand in front of him, refusing to back down this time. "I know how it feels to be willing to do anything to get out."

"See? You're willing to do anything to get out, but you're not my enemy?" He shook his head. "How does that make any fucking sense?"

She sighed, lowering her tone, showing him how resigned she felt. "Jace, we both know that at this point, I could never hurt you." The longer she was around him, the more she saw his reactions to her, the more sure she was.

"You expect me to believe that, Axie? You say it in that nice sweet voice, pout that bottom lip of yours, and I'm supposed to believe whatever comes out of your mouth?"

"We both know what's happening here between us." She climbed onto the bench at the foot of the bed so she could meet his glare head on. "And no amount of clenching your jaw or seething in a corner or pushing me away or screaming in my face is going to change it. You can fight men like my father, you can fight the guys that want to take your old man's throne, you can fight your brother. But you can't fight the universe. You can't fight fate."

"Yeah?" He reached out, grabbed her by the shoulders, picked her up, and tossed her onto the mattress with ease. "Fucking watch me, baby." He walked out, slamming the door behind him.

Axie screamed into her pillow.

Chapter Twenty-Two
Jace

Jace smiled as he heard her scream at the door he'd slammed shut. He knew it wasn't funny. None of this was fucking funny. But her reaction, her anger, he liked it. He liked when she jumped up on the bench to make her point, he liked the way her tiny fists clenched in front of her. Jace found that he was starting to enjoy most things Axie did, when she wasn't lying to his face.

After the meeting with his pack, he'd headed up stairs to her room without thought. He'd opened her door, and he'd watched her crying into her pillow. He didn't feel sorry for her, but he did *feel* for her. When she looked up, her eyes bright with tears, he knew the real reason he hadn't been able to sleep last night. His shifter had been restless, because he needed to make sure she was okay. And Jace had refused him.

But as exhaustion was taking over his brain and sobs were wracking Axie's small body, he'd decided to give in. For a few hours at least.

"What was that noise?" Baze came out of the kitchen, a dishtowel over his shoulder. "Is someone screaming?"

Jace stepped down the last step, breezing past him. "Axie."

"Is she hurt?" Baze followed him.

"No." Jace stopped short when he saw the giant fucking mess Baze had made of his state-of-the-art kitchen. "What happened in here?" It looked like every pot he owned was out, and dirty. There was flour on the floor and grease on the tile backsplash. "Did you try to cook?"

"Pen was hungry, and I couldn't find you."

Jace turned around, biting his lips together to keep from laughing at how defeated his alpha sounded. "Okay." He went to the fridge, searching for something that Baze hadn't already managed to waste or burn. "You clean, and I'll cook. I need to feed Axie anyway."

Baze went to the sink, turning on the hot water and pouring an absurd amount of dish soap into a large pot. "You *need* to feed her, huh?"

Had he said "need"? He hadn't meant to. Because that was some mate bullshit right there, and she wasn't his mate. Never would be. Jace shrugged. "She's my prisoner, my responsibility."

"Is that what she is? Your prisoner?"

Baze wasn't using his alpha tone, he was using the soft caring tone. His concerned father tone, the one that made Jace uncomfortable. "Thanks to your foray into cooking, we're out of food." He pulled a few ingredients out of the fridge and then closed it harder than necessary. "Looks like we're having grilled cheese and tomato soup."

"You avoiding my questions?"

"Yep." Jace got a loaf of bread out of the pantry, taking the skillet Baze cleaned and setting it on the stove.

"Well, then I'm avoiding the dishes." Baze turned off the water, wiping his hands on a towel. "Let us know when dinner is ready." He walked out, patting Jace on the back.

He sighed, switching on the burner, suddenly feeling like he needed another nap. He set about making enough sandwiches to feed six people, then opened a can of tomato soup. He hung his head, bracing his hands on the island and allowing himself a minute of peace and solitu—

"Why so broody, bro?" Jasper came into the kitchen, stealing a slice of cheese from the package as he hopped up on the counter. "Is it because more people want to kill us?"

He straightened, rolling his eyes, his typical response to most of his twin's antics. "Do you ever take anything fucking seriously?"

"What? Yes. I can seriously see that you're in here stewing." He waggled his eyebrows. "Your little prisoner being a bad girl? I heard her screaming a few minutes ago."

"I'm gonna hit you. This isn't a game."

"I know that, but does everything have to be so gloomy all the damn time?" Jasper tossed his hands up, letting them fall back to his thighs. "We're stuck in this house together, again. You think I want to be here? You think I want to watch you hack away at the sexual tension between you and Axie? Trying to dissolve it into thin air? I don't want to be here. I want to be out there, living my life, having fun."

Jasper noticed the tension between him and Axie? He thought his twin was oblivious to it, only thinking about his own dick. Had anyone else picked up on it? Not that it mattered, because she wasn't meant to be his, and he was going to keep his hands to himself.

From now on.

This afternoon didn't count.

Oh, or last night.

From this moment forward, he was going to keep his hands to himself.

And Jasper was right, he didn't ask for this, he didn't ask to be here again. A prisoner for his own safety. "I'm sorry. I'm sorry that you were dragged into all this again, that you have to stay cooped up in this house."

"It's not your fault, Jace." He held his arms out, his forearms on display. "You know, it doesn't matter how little I knew him, Franklin blood still runs through my veins and I guess that means there's a target on my back too." He reached over, dipping his finger into the butter container and eating a scoop of it. "I get it. They think we want his empire, and we just gotta figure out a way to convince them that we don't. That's all."

That's all. Like it was going to be easy convincing ruthless criminals of anything.

Jace turned off the two burners he'd been using, resting his back against the opposite counter. "I knew that after he was gone, someone else would take his place. I knew that we'd always need to be careful. I knew that there were a dozen other men as evil as Franklin waiting in the wings. But I didn't think it would get this bad. I thought if we kept our heads down and stayed away from everything he had, then they would leave us alone." He snorted, annoyed with himself. "I was stupid, naïve."

"No." Jasper's tone became hard, all playfulness gone. "What you were was hopeful and optimistic. Which I know are difficult emotions for you to pretend, let alone feel. You know, with all your gloom-and-doom bullshit, I worry. I know I joke around a lot and it doesn't seem like I take any of this serious." He reached out, putting his hands on Jace's shoulders. "But I need you to know that if I could take this from you, if I could carry this weight, and give you the life you never got to have, I would do it. I really would, man. You're my brother."

Jace stared at him, completely at a loss. He wasn't sure anyone had ever said anything so kind to him, so meaningful.

"It's all right, what I said doesn't need a response." Jasper laughed, lightening the mood like he was always doing. "I know you love me."

Jace was silent as Jasper grabbed one of the finished sandwiches and made his way out of the kitchen. Right before he was too late, Jace was finally able to speak. "I do, you know. I do love you."

"Like I said, I know."

Chapter Twenty-Three
Jace

Everyone ate in their rooms, or in other parts of the house, which wasn't usually the case. Jace had a large dining room table, and they typically ate there. But Riley and Jasper ate in the living room where they were in the middle of some Netflix binge. Pen wasn't feeling well, so Baze took their food upstairs so she wouldn't have to eat alone.

Jace stared at the pile of sandwiches and the pot of tomato soup before he decided to give in and take some up to Axie's room.

He didn't bother knocking, he simply opened the door and strolled in with their tray of food and a bottle of his most expensive whiskey. It was a peace offering, and a way to ensure that his shifter would let him sleep through the night.

"Hungry?"

"No." She picked up the remote beside her, clicking off whatever she'd been watching. "Go away, I can't handle anymore whiplash tonight."

He deserved that. But she'd been the one to break his trust. She'd been the one who set out to betray him and his friends. "No more whiplash." Jace sat the tray on the bed, uncapping the crystal decanter and passing it to her. "At least until the sun comes up."

She snorted, taking the bottle from him. "You think I'm going to let you stay in here tonight, you're fucking high."

"You'll let me stay in here." Jace picked up a sandwich, taking a large bite. "You can't deny me anything, we both know it. You said it yourself." She'd said it before he walked out on her.

"I think what I actually said was, I wouldn't be able to *hurt* you." She took a swig, wiping her mouth with the back of her hand. "I'll have no trouble *denying* you."

"We'll see." He held his sandwich in front of her. "Now eat." He hid his smile when she took a reluctant bite. He wanted to gloat, to point out that she was already unable to deny him. But he wasn't stupid, so he kept his mouth shut.

They ate in silence, passing the bottle of whiskey back and forth between them. After all three sandwiches were gone and Axie had all but drunk the whole bowl of tomato soup, he climbed off the bed.

"Where are you going? Time for the cold portion of your hot and cold attitude?"

He rolled his eyes, holding his hand out. "Come on, let's get ready for bed."

"Oh." She licked those perfect pouty lips of hers and got to her feet, walking past him and his hand.

Jace brushed his teeth with one of the spare toothbrushes he kept under all the sinks. Axie washed her face, removing all the makeup that was hiding her bruises. He sat on the edge of the soaker tub, watching her every move. He hated that she'd been hurt. He hated that he could still see another male's handprint on her throat. He waited while she brushed her teeth, her hair. When she was done, she turned to face him, leaning against the sink with her arms crossed protectively over her chest.

"What now?" She took a deep breath, her chest expanding. She wasn't being sarcastic. She was unsure of him, which made two of them. Like last night, Jace wasn't completely in control. His shifter was the reason he'd brought her food, the reason he knew he'd only sleep if she was curled up beside him.

Jace stood, taking her face in his hands. "Don't move, okay?"

She nodded.

He pressed his lips to the bruise under her eye, the ones on her throat. Then he dropped down to his knees, lifting her shirt to kiss her ribs, each mark a deep purple today. He closed his eyes, resting his head against her stomach. He was shaking, his wolf outraged that someone had hurt her this way, and that he had been powerless to stop it.

Axie ran her fingers through his hair, the motion soothing the chaos inside of him. "Hey." She used her hold on him to tilt his face up to hers. "You missed one." She pointed to her lips, like she had last night, with a smile on her beautiful face.

Jace stood to his full height, fully prepared to place one soft kiss on her lips and then step away. But the moment his mouth touched hers he lost his goddamn mind. He grabbed her ass, lifting her off the sink, growling in appreciation when her legs wound around his waist. He took the kiss deeper, his tongue dancing with hers, stealing the moans coming out of her mouth.

Jace walked them out of the bathroom, his mouth never leaving hers, then he laid her on the bed, nipping at her hipbone while he pulled her pants and panties off in one quick motion. He wanted...he needed to taste her, to hear her scream his name. He wanted to make her come, to make her happy. His shifter was demanding he touch her, tease her, have her.

Her hand went to his head when his teeth grazed her clit, pulling at his dark hair, asking for more without using words. Jace smiled against her mound, loving that she wanted this as much as he did. He slipped one finger inside her hot, wet core, pumping in and out, keeping a relentless rhythm as he ran his tongue over her sweet, soft flesh.

"Fuck, Jace, don't stop."

He growled against her clit, his chest vibrating from the sound, his shifter eating up her words as he drew in the scent of her. He lapped at her center, drawing her closer and closer to the edge. He didn't have it in him to slow them down, to savor the moment. He needed to bring her to the edge and make her dive over. He could feel her body start to tighten, like a coil about to snap. He flicked his tongue against her clit at the same time he added a second finger inside her pussy. Axie screamed out his name, and he kept at her, drawing her orgasm out like a tidal wave.

Her breaths were coming out in soft pants while her fingers still twisted in his hair. Jace stayed between her perfect thighs, licking her until she was clean.

By the time he felt sated enough to stop, Axie was sound asleep.

Chapter Twenty-Four
Axie

Axie opened her eyes to pitch black, It had to be the middle of the night. But why in the hell was she so damn hot? She went to throw the heavy blanket off her body but didn't get very far. She was blocked by Jace's leg and an arm. He was draped over her, on top of the covers, pinning her to the mattress and giving her one hell of an epic hot flash.

She sighed, flopping back down to her pillow. What did she do now? She didn't want to wake him up. She knew there was a good chance that if she did that, he'd turn back into cold asshole Jace and leave her to go back to his own room. And as much as she hated to admit it, she didn't want that to happen.

He'd surprised her tonight. It wasn't the wicked things he'd done to her pussy with his mouth, though he was so good at it, he'd knocked her out. That he was still in her bed was the shocker. Well that, and she was pretty sure he'd acknowledged their connection. Which meant maybe she wasn't crazy, seeing signs that weren't there.

Her mind was spinning, but at the moment she needed to get these covers off and find a way to turn down the air without disturbing the sleeping shifter beside her.

Axie grabbed the edge of the mattress, using it to help pull her body out from under Jace. She slid slowly away until she could slither like a human snake down to the floor. And then for added stealth mode, she crawled on her hands and knees to the bedroom door before finally getting to her feet and unlocking it. She kept her eyes on Jace, making sure that the sound didn't wake him.

Now that she wasn't lying underneath him, and that pile of blankets, she was feeling better. But she still wanted to turn down the AC, because she knew that the second she got back in bed he'd cling to her again. And she was more than okay with that.

"What are you doing?"

Axie jumped about a foot in the air, whirling around with her hand on her chest. "What in the flying fuck, guys? Why are you creeping around the hallway in the dark? Together?" She reached out and shoved at Jasper's shoulder when he started to laugh, her heart still firmly in her throat.

"Us?" Riley snorted quietly. "You're the one who ghosted out of your room."

She opened her mouth to correct him that it wasn't her room: it was her prison. And that she wasn't a guest. Jace had demanded she stay here. But she couldn't seem to make the words form, because they weren't altogether true. Not anymore.

"I was looking for the thermostat. I'm burning up." She peered around, hoping she'd see the control panel.

"It's run from an app we have on our phones." Jasper held up his cell to show her. "How cold you want it, gorgeous?"

"Arctic." She fanned her still flushed face. "Sleeping next to Jace is like sleeping with a heater."

Riley looked past her, into the bedroom she'd snuck out of where the door was still open a bit. "You were with Jace?"

She nodded. "Yeah, why?"

"Did he touch you?" Riley stepped back, his gaze widening as he noticed the giant shirt she was wearing over her bare legs. "Did you guys, um, mess around?"

Axie narrowed her eyes, wrinkling her nose. "Now you two really are being creepy. Why would you ask me that? I figured you guys were into some kink when you were prepared to share me that first night, but wanting to know the details of what Jace and I were doing while we're standing around in the dark together? Too much guys, even for me."

Riley rolled his eyes, his face lit up by Jasper's cell phone. "We don't want details, it's—"

"Speak for yourself." Jasper crossed his arms over his muscled chest, a smirk on his face. "I'd be down to hear what's been happening between you and my twin in there." He winked. "Did you pretend it was me? We look alike, you know."

Riley pushed Jasper to the side, but he was slow to uncross his arms so he ended up falling to the ground in a hilarious heap. Axie couldn't help but start to laugh. She covered her mouth, trying to keep quiet. "You deserved that, you weirdo. And you and Jace actually don't look all that much alike."

"Axie, focus." Riley snapped his fingers in front of her face. "Did you and Jace hook up?"

She held her index finger and thumb close together. "Little bit." She started fanning her face again. She really needed the air to kick on soon. "We didn't have sex or anything, not that it's any of your business. Why am I even answering you?" She sighed, pulling Jace's t-shirt away from her body and using it to try to get some air circulating. "It's because I'm so hot, I can't think clearly."

"You smell good." Jasper was still on the ground. He'd crawled closer to her, his nose lined up with her stomach. "Riley, do you smell that?"

"Fuck." Riley grabbed Jasper by his shirt and tossed him back away from her, putting himself between the two of them. "Jasper, get out of here." When Jasper moved to step toward her instead, Riley threw his arm out. "Goddamnit."

"What's happening?" Axie pressed herself to the wall, unnerved by the way Jasper seemed to be fighting to get to her. "What's wrong with him?"

"He's reacting to you, to your scent. You're not just overheated, it's your body craving the bond." Riley had both his hands on Jasper's chest now.

Her heart was starting to beat wildly, which was only making her grow hotter. She wanted to go downstairs and lie in the cool grass in the backyard. "What are you talking about?"

"Don't do that. I can't have both you *and* Jace burying your heads in the sand and pretending like this isn't happening. Your body wants Jace to finish what he started, and Jasper has proved to be a little sensitive to this sort of thing in the past."

What Riley was saying didn't make all that much sense, but she wasn't about to argue when she needed to stick her head in the nearest freezer. "I'll go downstairs." Jace had been sleeping on top of her, that's why she was feeling this way. There were so many blankets. This had nothing to do with her body wanting to be claimed by the shifter in her bed. Sure, their connection was undeniable. But she wasn't a shifter, her body was her own, she was in control.

"Axie, don't fucking move." Riley shook his head, trying to walk Jasper backward toward the staircase. "Don't try to pass him, go back to your room, lock the door." He sounded like he was straining, using all his strength to keep his friend from charging her.

"Come on, man, can't you feel that? She wants me, she wants *us*." Jasper licked his lips and Axie felt along the wall, trying to locate the doorknob without turning her back to them. "We can share her, you heard her. She was good with it."

"No, snap out of it, you stupid horn-dog." Riley kept pushing, his feet barely gaining any purchase on the waxed wooden floors. "Dammit, Jasper."

Her body hit air, the wall suddenly disappearing and causing her to stumble. But Jace caught her, his arm snaking around her middle as he shoved her behind him. He was growling, the sound coming from deep in his chest. She rested her forehead on his back, loving that his hand stayed on her lower back, pressing her against him.

"Get him out of here." Jace's tone was low, but commanding. "Before I fucking kill him."

"I'm trying." Riley got down low, trying to use his whole body to move Jasper. "I could use a little help here."

"I can't. I'll hurt him. I won't be able to stop." Jace's chest was heaving, his body vibrating, he was shimmering before Axie's eyes. He was fighting his shift, she could tell. "Baze." He called down the hallway, raising his voice in a way that made the hairs on the back of her neck stand on end. "Baze."

A door opened and closed. She couldn't see anything though. Jace was holding her immobile. "Why are you all in the hallway? It's the middle of the fuck...Riley? Why are you fighting with Jasper?"

"Axie, she uh, remember those hot flashes Maddi had before she and Linc sealed the deal?" Riley gestured with his head to his friend, the one he was still trying to hold in place. "Jasper can't resist, if you know what I mean."

This whole time, Jasper had been silently trying to get to her. He wasn't raging, he wasn't yelling. He was simply in a relentless pursuit to get to her.

"Get him out of here, Baze." Jace was still shaking, his hand now fisted in Axie's shirt. "Get him downstairs, the basement, somewhere far away from me." His eyes were on the ground, like he couldn't even handle looking at his twin. "Now."

Axie finally saw Baze step into view, joining Riley. He reared back and punched Jasper in the face. He fell to the ground, out cold by the time Baze turned around to address her and Jace. "Someone want to explain what in the actual fuck is going on?"

Riley dropped his hands to his knees, breathing heavy like he was exhausted from keeping Jasper away from her for so long.

"No." Jace backed up, moving her farther into the room with his body. But when he went to close their door, Riley's fist flew out, stopping it. Jace snarled, "Now's not the time, Riley. I'll kill you just as easily."

Would he? Would he really have killed his twin and his best friend?

"Then fucking kill me," Riley yelled, gesturing at the guy on the ground. "You have us all locked in this house, you can't hide what's happening. You can't wish it away. You know where that leads, we all know, we've seen it. Someone will get hurt, it could be one of us, or it could be Axie. What if I hadn't been here? What if Baze hadn't been here to help me?" Riley shook his head. "One of us wouldn't have made it out alive."

Jace stayed silent as Baze's gaze swung to him, his eyes getting big when he noticed her standing behind him. "What's going on, kid?"

Axie had only heard Baze speak once, down at the pack meeting, but the tone he was using with Jace now was different. It was soft, pleading, like a parent who simply wanted to know what was going on. But still, Jace kept quiet.

"She's his, she's Jace's." Riley answered for him, no longer yelling. "Don't bother trying to talk to him about it though, he's still convinced the universe made a mistake."

Holy shit. Hearing those words out loud was jarring.

"It did, it did make a mistake." Jace turned, gently pushing her into the room they'd shared. "Good night." He kicked the door shut, and surprisingly, he wasn't on the other side of it.

She'd fully expected him to leave her in here alone, to put distance between them. Like Riley said, Jace believed the universe

124

had made a mistake. He'd even convinced her that she was losing her mind, that everything she was experiencing was one-sided.

She whispered, afraid to spook him, "I thought you'd walk away, after what happened with Jasper."

Jace stepped closer to her, his hands going to her face. "I want to, so bad. But my shifter won't let me." He kissed her lips, stealing the air from her lungs as his hand moved down to her ass. He lifted her, laying her on the bed. "You were in danger, again, and he's not going to let me go anywhere." He rested his forehead on her chest. "I'm sorry."

His whispered words, and the desperation in his tone... He was breaking her heart.

"No, I'm sorry." She ran her fingers through his hair. "I'm sorry I fucked up your life. I'm sorry I make things so hard for you. I'm sorry I cause problems between you and your brother."

He rolled off her body, spooning her with his front pressed to her back. This seemed to be his favorite way to sleep, to hold her. And she loved that it was becoming familiar. Jace kissed her jaw, her neck, his teeth grazing the sensitive space between her throat and her shoulder. His fingers threaded through her hair, gently brushing out the long strands. He alternated little nips at her skin, taking away the sting every time with his soft kisses.

He didn't speak words to reassure her that they were going to be okay.

But she fell asleep feeling content and cared for nonetheless.

Chapter Twenty-Five
Jace

Jace had been awake for at least an hour, lying in bed beside Axie, wracking his brain for all the right things to say when she finally opened her striking green eyes. He knew pushing her away again was futile. It'd only last until the sun went down, and then his shifter would demand that he come climb in bed with her. And if he resisted, he wouldn't get any sleep. He needed sleep. He needed his mind functioning on all cylinders if he was going to figure a way out of the mess they were in. Men were after information, and soon they'd get frustrated and be out for blood instead. That's what Franklin would do. That's what he'd taught Jace to do.

And Riley was right. Last night was a cluster fuck. When he'd heard Riley outside, his voice raised in near panic, he'd shot out of bed. He'd never felt so close to an instinctual shift in all his life. Even as a young kid, he'd always had more control than most. But when he saw Jasper fighting to get to Axie, it took all the strength he possessed to restrain himself. He wanted to lash out. He wanted to truly kill his twin for the first time in his life.

"How long have you been watching me sleep?" Axie rolled over, burying her face against his shoulder. "Why is everyone in this house so creepy?"

He turned on his side, resting his head on his arm. "You want to talk about last night?"

"What? Did hell freeze over? Are there pigs flying around outside?" She moved back so they were face-to-face. "Because I feel like all those things would happen before you voluntarily spoke to me about last night. Or anything for that matter."

She had a point. Avoidance was the name of his game. But he really didn't want to rip his brother's head clean off his body, so certain conversations needed to be had. "There is a Latin phrase for what you were feeling, and please don't tell Pen I can't for the life of me remember what it is."

"Who is Pen?"

Jesus. He really had kept her at a distance, hadn't he? She'd been in his home for close to forty-eight hours and she had no clue who anyone was. "I'll introduce you to her today." She nodded, pulling her bottom lip through her teeth. "Don't do that, it makes my shifter feel antsy."

"Is antsy a nice way of saying horny?"

He smiled despite himself. "Yes."

"Jace, what Riley said last night, about us." She hesitated, which wasn't like her. "He's right, isn't he?"

Jace reached out and brushed a lock of hair off her forehead. "About you being mine?" She nodded, her eyes searching his. "Yes."

Axie started to lick her lips, but stopped herself, smiling instead. "The night we met, every touch other than yours felt wrong. And when we were in the car on the way home, I wanted you. I wanted to curl into a ball on your lap and never leave." He stayed silent, unsure of the perfect thing to say. Luckily, she kept talking, saving him. "But you kept pushing me away, so I started to question myself, and everything I was feeling."

He sighed, recognizing the frustration behind her words. "I never wanted a mate, Axie. I never thought I'd have one. So when my wolf reacted so strongly to you, I fought it. I thought if I didn't touch you, didn't kiss you, I could stop whatever had started between us." He shrugged. "But you can't fight fate."

She gasped dramatically. "You can't? Oh wow. How insightful. The person who told you that must be fucking brilliant." Jace snorted, but otherwise stayed quiet because she was right. "You talk about your shifter like it's a separate part of you. I've never heard anyone else do that before."

Jace moved the hair off her neck to admire his handiwork. She was covered with his mark, which drove his next point home. "My shifter and I don't really seem to agree on much, so yeah, I feel like we're two different beings."

"Why don't you two get along?" She trailed her fingers down his arm, tickling his skin and causing goosebumps to erupt.

"I like control and he seems to invite chaos at every chance he gets." Jace traced Axie's face, checking her bruises and cuts. "Like you. You are straight chaos, and he's super into you."

"But Jace isn't." She said the words softly, like they wounded her and she didn't want him to know.

Jace wanted to hold back, to keep his feelings to himself. But it seemed that the other part of him, the more primal part, was in the driver's seat more and more every second. Yesterday morning, it was easy to stay away from Axie. Then after he saw her at the pack meeting, he'd followed her upstairs without much thought. Last night brought them closer, in more ways than one. Little by little, his shifter was winning this fight. And he knew that one day, he'd have to give in. He'd claim her, he'd take what was meant to be his. So it made sense, he supposed, to let her in.

"It's hard for me to trust, to open up."

"And I lied to you." Axie's gaze became fixed on his chest.

"You did." He put his finger under her chin, lifting her face. "But you had your reasons, reasons I can appreciate. And I believe you when you say that you'd never be able to hurt me now."

"You do? Why?"

"Because I could never hurt you either." He kissed her forehead.

"Pushing me away hurts. Putting distance between us hurts."

"No, it pissed you off. It frustrated you, which was why I was able to walk away." His kissed the bruise under her eye, the one from her father. "Last night, I knew leaving you alone after what happened with Jasper would hurt. So I stayed. I had no choice. I knew if you woke up alone this morning, it would hurt, so I lay in bed and watched you sleep." He kissed the cut on her lip. "I can't push you away anymore."

"Your shifter won't let you."

"No, he won't." He placed one final kiss on each fingerprint around her throat. "But now I'm hungry, and I need a whole pot of coffee. Which means we need to talk about what's going on with your body so we can go downstairs and have breakfast."

Axie laughed, the sweet sound filling the room. "I feel like I'm about to get one of those puberty pep talks that the parents give on an after-school special."

"The only reason I know anything about any of this is because I've seen it before, and because Pen teaches history of shifter culture at St. Leasing. She's like an encyclopedia on all things supernatural. Like I said, there's a name for it, and it translates to like heat seeking or something. It's your body craving mine, calling to mine."

"Are you serious? I want your dick so bad that my body is spazzing out?" She narrowed her eyes, like she didn't believe she'd been so clueless until now.

He had to fight the urge to prove to her how spot on her incredulous assessment was. The word dick coming out of pouty lips wasn't helping anything either. "You want the bond to be complete."

"Now I can see where you're coming from with you and your shifter not really agreeing all the time. I don't carry the gene, but I'm not really on the same page as my body at the moment."

Axie didn't want to be mated to him. That's what she was telling him. And he hated how it caused a sharp pain in his chest. But then again, why would she want to belong to him? All he had shown her this whole fucking time was anger.

Jace needed time. He needed to get to know the girl the universe had created to be his. He had to show her that he could be kind, that he wouldn't push her away anymore. "There are ways we can work around it, prolong the process." He'd seen it work with Linc and Maddi. It had bought them the time they needed for her to be ready.

"Okay good, how do we do that?"

"Well, you need to pay close attention to how you're feeling." Maddi had said that she could feel it coming, like it started out small and then it would build until it took over her whole body. "If you start to get hot, get to a room with a lock on the door. Keep your phone with you and call me. If you can't get hold of me, call Baze."

"The guy from last night? The alpha?"

"Yes. Pen and Baze are mated, and they live here with me. They're like my family, I guess. I trust them. They'll take care of you." Jace felt like such an asshole for not bothering to introduce Axie to anyone when they were at the house yesterday. But twenty-four hours ago he'd still been convinced that he could stop what was happening. And maybe he could have, if his shifter hadn't demanded he bury his face between her legs last night.

"What else can we do? To, you know, put off the rest of our lives?"

In that moment, Jace realized for the first time how young Axie looked without any makeup on, his shirt falling off her shoulder.

He'd never gotten to be a child. He didn't get the chance to grow up slowly. But she did. She was an eighteen-year-old girl, thrust into a life that she wasn't prepared for. She'd spent the last year planning to run away from her father, from Colorado, from her life in a shifter family. And now she was in a bed that wasn't hers with a guy she'd just met, surrounded by people she didn't know.

Jace had been so focused on what he wanted and what he didn't that his anger, and his irrationality prevented him from thinking about how unsettled Axie must have been feeling. He'd finish telling her what she needed to know and then he'd take her downstairs and introduce her to his family.

"To complete the bond, we need to have sex."

Axie nodded. "You have to come inside me, nothing between us."

For fucks sake. Was she trying to make this hard on him? He reached under the covers and discreetly adjusted his cock.

"Yes." He took a deep breath, trying to calm all the blood rushing to his dick. "And as long as we don't do that one particular thing, then we should be okay for a little while."

"A little while?"

"It's not an exact science, Axie. We're all figuring it out as we go. But doing things that way worked for Linc and Maddi, two other mated members of my pack." He didn't think it was necessary to add that it only worked until one of his father's henchmen tried to rape her and Linc lost his fucking mind. "We go slow, take our time, manage the symptoms as they come."

"Symptoms as in plural? They don't pass out pamphlets on this crap in public school."

"Come on, that's enough learning for one morning." He wasn't about to get into the extreme pain they could both experience. "I need coffee."

Chapter Twenty-Six
Axie

Jace stayed in bed while she showered, taking her time and standing under the hot spray to ease the tight muscles in her body. She didn't know if the soreness she was feeling was left over from the asshole who grabbed her, or all the stress of the last twenty-four hours.

Yesterday had been difficult and frustrating. She'd felt alone and irritated. When Jace had walked out on her after their nap, she'd thought she'd reached her breaking point, screaming into her pillow until she was hoarse. But he'd been right this morning. She hadn't been hurt. Pissed, with a dash of hopelessness.

Axie knew from day one that there was something altogether different about her reaction to Jace Franklin. At first, she'd dismissed it, thinking maybe she wanted him because he didn't want her. She was an eighteen-year-old smoke show. She wasn't above cliché behavior like that. Clearly, she put a BAND-AID on his rejection by letting his brother and best friend put their hands all over her body.

But then when it kept happening, when Jace could easily toss her aside like she didn't matter to him at all, she started to wonder if she was wrong, if she was losing her mind. After last night, there was no denying it anymore. She wasn't crazy, and Jace wasn't immune to her. Or at least, his shifter wasn't. It didn't hurt her feelings that Jace and his shifter weren't on the same page when it came to their future. She was having dueling emotions about it too. She was fucking eighteen, on her way out of this stupid town. She had plans. She wanted to feel free. She wanted to be wild, without anyone to answer to for once in her goddamn life. But apparently the universe didn't give two shits about what she wanted for herself, huh?

Axie knew you couldn't fight fate, which was exactly what she'd told Jace. She was raised in a shifter household. She knew the score.

Her parents had been true mates, and when Axie had been a little girl, her mother had told her all about their love story. She'd lie awake in bed, listening to her mom speak about her father like her mom was telling her a fairy tale. When her mom got sick and passed away, Axie cried herself to sleep every night, terrified that her father would die too from a broken heart. But no. His heart didn't break. It hardened until it was unrecognizable.

She sighed, refusing to think about her father right now. Jace was finally being nice to her and she wasn't going to ruin her good mood by bringing her father into it. She shut off the water and wrapped a fluffy gray towel around her body, turning when the door slowly swung open, letting all the heat start to escape.

"You take long showers." Jace was leaning against the wall, his arms crossed over his bare chest. He was so ridiculously sexy. Dark and built, his jawline could cut her lines of coke. "I *need* coffee."

She glanced at her cell where it sat on the counter. "I was in there for less than ten minutes." She faced the mirror, wiping away the steam so she could quickly get dressed.

"Hurry." He came to stand behind her, moving her wet hair to the side and placing a sweet kiss on her neck. "And don't even try to cover those up." He met her eyes in the mirror, then walked back into the bedroom.

She leaned forward, looking closer at her skin. *Motherfucker.* "You marked me?" Was that what he'd been doing last night as she fell asleep? It'd felt so good that she hadn't cared, as long as he didn't stop. But now she looked like she had a weird disease. "There are bites and like, are those hickeys? Are you kidding me?"

"I won't claim you, neither of us are ready for that." He was talking from the bed, where he was once again lying as he typed away on his phone. "My shifter and I compromised."

Compromised her ass. He'd marked her body outside, since he couldn't, well, *mark* her inside. There were those dueling reactions she'd learned to welcome when it came to Jace. She was pissed and extremely turned on at the same time. Axie braced her hands on the sink, closing her eyes and taking a few deep breaths.

We should be okay for a little while. Manage the symptoms as they come.

Was this what he'd meant, that it would become increasingly difficult not to mount him?

"You okay in there?"

She glanced into her room, which was a damn mistake. Jace was propped up on his elbows, his abs flexed and on full display. She nodded, tearing her eyes away from him as she swung the door closed. "Yep. I'm good." There, she wouldn't look at him and everything would be fucking fine.

"Axie, are you feeling hot? Flushed? If you feel it coming, you can't go downstairs. You can't be around unbonded males."

"I'm fine." She whipped her brush through her hair, before pinning the wet locks on top of her head. She didn't have the bandwidth to put effort into her appearance right now. "Not going into heat." Because that was pretty much what it was, right? Her body demanding his and sending a fucking signal to all the other shifters in the vicinity, like a dog in heat.

She pulled on the short shorts and lightweight long-sleeve shirt she'd brought in with her, not trusting herself to change in the other room with Jace. He was too tempting this morning, being nice to her like he cared. Typical chick with daddy issues right there, she rolled her eyes at herself.

When she finally opened the door, he was across the room, standing at the window with his hands resting on the top of his head. Which made his arms look seriously carved.

He turned when he heard her. "You ready? My stomach is eating itself."

"Don't be so dramatic." She opened the door, stepping into the hallway only to be pulled back into the bedroom. "Uh, I thought you were *starving*?"

Jace let go of her arm and then left the room, speaking over his shoulder, "I am, but I need you to walk behind me."

"Oh, hell to the no." Axie jogged a few steps until she was in front of him again. "You think I'm going to spend the rest of my life letting you put me beneath you? Like I'm less than you?" She yelped when his arms snaked around her waist, spinning and depositing her behind him once again.

"Now who is being dramatic?" He stood in front of her, power stance on point. "I don't want Jasper to jump out of the shadows and try to fuck you."

"Oh." She licked her lips, feeling a little silly for her outburst. "In that case, go ahead." Thankfully, he didn't call her out any further and simply turned to make his way down the stairs, with her behind him.

He was holding her hand, which she thought was sweet until he dropped it the second he realized the kitchen was empty. His contact hadn't been about how much his human side was starting to like her; it'd been about protecting her from shifter threats.

Axie sat on one of the stools at the island, watching as Jace moved around the kitchen, stretching to reach into cabinets, his forearms flexing as he made coffee. Was she drooling? She wiped at her mouth to be sure. She'd appreciated how attractive Jace was from the moment she'd laid eyes on him: there was no way not to. But this morning, it was like every feature was amplified to make her *want* him. Was this a symptom? Must be. She usually had much more chill than this.

"How do you like it?"

Reckless and a lot like a vigorous workout.

She shook her head, not allowing her original answer to come out. "Huh?"

"Your coffee." Jace let a small smile show, like he knew exactly where her mind had gone when he asked her that question. Was he playing with her? Flirting? She didn't know he was capable.

"Cream and sugar, more cream than sugar." She put her hands on the island, prepared to stand and make it herself. But Jace started to growl, the sound carrying through the kitchen like a vibration. Axie glance behind her to see Jasper.

He held his hands up, like he was trying to placate his brother. "Jace, I'm fine now, I swear." He stepped cautiously into the room. "Think about it. You've seen it happen with Maddi. You know if Axie is feeling normal, I'm not a threat. You *know* this." Jasper met her eyes briefly. "You feel okay, Ax?"

She nodded, secretly liking how he and Riley called her Ax like they had been friends for years instead of days.

"See? We're all good, I'd never intentionally hurt her or you." Jasper took a deep breath, then rose to his full height and opened the fridge. He was going for casual, trying to force Jace to calm down. But the tension in the room was still tangible.

Jace hadn't moved, he was rigid, his chest heaving, his eyes tracking Jasper's every action. He still had the creamer in his hand, two steaming mugs of coffee sitting next to him on the counter. Axie darted her gaze between the two shifters, not entirely sure what to do. She didn't want to make things worse, for either of them. And sometimes it seemed like she could make a wrong move in this house by simply existing.

"Go to him." Axie wasn't sure who that voice belonged to, but she did what they told her because she certainly didn't have the answer.

She got off her stool, walking around the island the opposite direction of where Jasper was standing with the fridge still open, drinking orange juice straight from the carton.

When Axie got within arm's reach of Jace, he grabbed her roughly, pulling her behind him.

"Jasper, get a glass." She peeked around Jace's back to see a pretty woman whack Jasper on the back of the head. "This whole house doesn't want your germs." That must be Pen, who Jace talked about this morning while they were lying in bed. She had blonde hair and kind eyes in a beautiful light brown color that Axie was instantly jealous of. "And then come sit over here so Jace can finish making their coffee before it's too cold to drink."

Jasper rolled his eyes but went and sat next to her anyway. "How long are we going to have to cater to Jace's bonded male bullshit?"

"Until he's actually a bonded male." Pen rested her chin in her hand. "Bubs, can I have a cup too, please?"

Bubs? Axie didn't think Jace was the kind of guy who would let people call him cutesy nicknames like that, so she couldn't help but giggle.

Thankfully, somewhere between Pen's request and Axie's soft laughter, Jace started to relax. The tension left his shoulders, and he stopped that pre-shift shimmer that he'd done last night too. He turned back to the counter, and Axie stepped to the side to get out of his way.

He met her eyes, his jaw still grinding. "You sure you feel okay?"

She nodded, going out on a limb and putting her hand on his chest, not entirely convinced he wouldn't shove it away now that they had an audience. "Promise." His attention went to her neck, his lips twitching like he wanted to smile at his mark again.

"Stay on this side of the island." It wasn't a request. He'd made a command. But she didn't want to be the cause of a bloodbath before breakfast, so she was fine with letting it slide.

"Okay." She accepted the warm mug he placed into her waiting hands, taking a deep inhale and appreciating the rich familiar scent. Her mother had loved coffee, had to have it the second she woke up. Axie had never enjoyed the taste, but she made it every morning without fail, because it reminded her of a better time. A time when she felt safe and loved.

Although, right now, she had to admit that she felt pretty fucking cared for.

Chapter Twenty-Seven
Jace

The kitchen was full now. For some reason, Jace didn't have the same reaction to Riley being in the room with Axie as he had with Jasper. His twin was sensitive when it came to the hot flashes that happened when people tried to prolong the bonding process. It'd happened with Maddi, and logically Jace knew that it wasn't Jasper's fault. He wasn't in control of his shifter any more than Jace was. That didn't mean that Jace didn't see him as a threat.

Jace would protect Axie. He'd protect what belonged to him, at all costs. And she did. Belong to him.

His shifter wouldn't allow him to deny it anymore, not after last night. He'd touched her. Hell, he'd more than touched her. He'd made her come, and his shifter had loved every fucking second of it. Almost as much as he'd loved marking her as she fell asleep in his arms.

"Jace, you still coming with us today?" Baze glanced to Riley and Jasper, who were on the opposite side of the kitchen from Axie. "To that, uh, meeting?"

"Well, that sounded sketch as hell," Jasper scoffed, clearly picking up on the fact that Baze was trying to talk in code.

Pen wasn't ready for anyone else to know she was pregnant. She still wasn't convinced that the baby was real. But Jace and Baze knew different, and he knew Riley did too when he kept his eyes on the counter and bit his lips together to keep from smiling.

Jasper could only feel Maddi's baby girl, because they were connected. Riley could sense the baby growing in Pen's small stomach because that was part of his supernaturalness. Riley was discreet though, and he'd never tell anyone until Pen and Baze were ready.

"Yeah." Jace finished his last bite of toast, talking as he chewed around it. "Axie and I will both come."

"Oh no. I don't want to impose on whatever *meeting* was code for." She shook her head. "I can stay here with Riley."

"No." Jace's voice came out rough, his throat sore from all the growling and snarling he'd been doing since Axie crashed into his life. She opened her mouth like she wanted to argue, to put him in his place, but he reached out and rubbed his hand on her lower back. The movement was hidden from everyone else in the kitchen, and it was gentle. He was silently asking her not to push him. And thankfully, she didn't.

"Are you worried about her being here with us?" Jasper pointed at Axie, and Jace fought the urge to rip his finger clean off. "We get it, we can't touch her." He chuckled lightly. "You marked her, you called dibs."

Axie covered the bites on her neck with her palm, her eyes shooting to his in annoyance. "He has you there."

Jace's lips twitched. They'd been doing that a lot this morning. He was happy, if not on edge. He kept wanting to smile, which wasn't something he did as often as everyone else. He enjoyed Axie's attitude about most things. It was like she went with the flow, but still felt the need to call people on their bullshit at the same time. If she was irritated, she said so. She was no match for his shifter, but she could sure as hell hold her own against his human side.

"So are we all just acknowledging this now? Axie is Jace's forever?" Jasper's eyes darted around the kitchen, as if he was truly looking for an answer.

Baze answered, "After last night, I don't think there is a whole hell of a lot left to say."

Jace agreed, and everyone else must have too because the kitchen stayed silent.

"Yeah." Jace figured now was as good a time as any to make sure there was no argument about how the day was going to go. "You're coming with us. If you have another hot flash, Riley won't be able to hold Jasper off without help." He worked to push past the newfound anger he felt remembering last night's disaster in the hallway. "A locked door won't stop him, and I'd never make it back here in time."

He wouldn't apologize for making her comply, but he compromised by at least sharing his reasoning. The more he gave in to his shifter, the better they seemed to work in tandem.

"I'm sorry, Ax." Jasper rested his elbows on the island, his head in his hands. "I wish it didn't affect me like it does. I hate that I scared you last night."

"It's okay, it's not your fault." Axie pursed her lips. "I mean, like, I accept your apology. I really have no clue if it's your fault or not because I don't know why it bothers you but not Rye."

Rye? For fucks sake.

"It's *mostly* not his fault." Pen smiled behind her coffee mug, savoring the one cup of caffeine she was allowed a day. "But some of it is." She had all their attention now. "When I started teaching my class at St. Leasing, I dove headfirst into research mode. I wanted to be able to answer any and all questions that came my way." She pointed to *Rye*. "Riley is chill, he's calm and not much seems to bother him, he's for sure the most compassionate of any shifter in this pack. His abilities mirror Baze's. They can both pick up on subtle changes in others, but his *personality* is more like Keller. Jasper on the other hand? He's like Linc, through and through. He's a player, a fuck boy. Because that's where his supernatural abilities lie."

Jasper winked playfully at Axie, and Jace couldn't help but reach across the table and flick him on the forehead. "Stop it."

Baze put his hands on Pen's shoulders, failing to hide the humor in his voice. "Makes perfect sense. It affects his shifter, because his shifter is perpetually searching for something to hump."

"I'm a healthy boy with a healthy sexual appetite." Jasper smiled around a mouth full of cereal. "There's nothing wrong with that, you know, until I try to fuck my brother's girl."

Everyone was silent except Jace, who was once again unable to hold in his snarl as he gripped Axie's hip protectively.

"Okay, well, we've got to leave soon or we'll be late." Pen got to her feet, breaking the newest round of tension in the room and pulling Baze out of the kitchen and up the stairs.

"When we get back, I want to go over the files Mathias sent over." Jace had gotten an email that morning while Axie had been in the shower, but he knew it'd take hours to go over everything

Mathias sent so he hadn't even bothered to open it. "And then, we'll get together and come up with a game plan."

"We?" Jasper took his bowl to the sink, rinsing it as he spoke over his shoulder. "You want our help? Our input?"

Jace nodded. "We're in this together, right?" It was his own way of extending an olive branch, of telling his brother that he forgave him for last night. That he knew that he'd never intentionally hurt him or his, uh, Axie.

Jace was an island. That was how he'd been raised. Over the last year or so, he'd been working hard to be less of an asshole. Most of the time, he failed and kept everyone at a distance. But today, with Axie pressed against his side, his twin doing the dishes, his best friend FaceTiming Hadley to tell her good morning even though she couldn't even talk yet, he felt somewhat *content*. Like all was right in the world if only for a moment, which normally only happened when he was alone with Penelope.

Maybe for once he could chase the peace instead of running from it.

"Yeah, man, of course we are." Jasper closed the dishwasher. "Come find us when you guys get home from Pen's doctor appointment."

"You know about that?" Jace raised his brows in surprise. Pen had hit the nail on the head when she was describing Jasper a few minutes ago. His shifter abilities had a one-track mind. He was shocked that Jasper figured it out on his own. "How could you tell?"

Jasper's attention darted to Riley, a smirk on his face and yet another wink in his eye. "Riley and I are good at sharing secrets and whatnot."

"What the hell, man?" Riley had gotten off the phone in time to hear Jasper tell on him. "I told you to keep your mouth shut until she was ready to tell everyone." He grabbed Jasper in a headlock, dragging him from the room. "I can't fucking tell you anything, can I?" The two of them disappeared into the living room, their laughter and roughhousing trailing behind them.

"So those two really do share."

Jace swung down, capturing Axie's lips and silencing her words. When he finally released her, he spoke against the shell of her ear. "I am not in the mood to listen to you ponder Riley and Jasper's sexual preferences, okay?"

She nodded, and gave him a wicked little smile.

"You still feeling okay?"

Her smile fell as she took and let out a deep breath like she was taking inventory of her body. "Internal temperature doesn't resemble fire and brimstone."

He patted her ass, pushing her in the direction of the stairs. "Go get changed, and meet me out front. We're taking one car. I don't want us spread out."

"Safety in numbers?"

She was staring up at him with her big eyes, and his shifter was starting to stir. He wanted her underneath them, whimpering, close to the edge. He took a step back, not trusting himself.

"I'm calmer when I'm in control."

It was the truth, and he'd shared it with her without an ounce of hesitation.

Chapter Twenty-Eight
Axie

The waiting room they were sitting in was cold as hell, which was good she supposed. It would help keep her body cool. Because Jace looked handsome as fuck and she was having a hard time not climbing into his lap and demanding he make her come. Maybe she was like Jasper and Linc, perpetually looking for something to hump. At least that was the way she felt today.

"Penelope Sutton?" A nurse in pink scrubs stood in an open doorway, a kind smile on her face.

Pen stood, smoothing down her black maxi dress like she was trying to soothe her nerves at the same time. Baze and Jace both got to their feet, Baze's hand going to Pen's lower back to guide her through the maze of chairs. Jace's hand reach down and grabbed her own, pulling her to her feet despite her protest.

"This is a family thing. It's a big deal." She tried to sit back down. "You guys go, there isn't much trouble I can get into here and I don't want to impose." It was easy for her to see how much Jace cared about Penelope. It was in their every interaction. He was never stern with her, always kind and soft. And even though Axie didn't have siblings, or anyone she was close to like these three were with each other, she understood the importance of today.

"You guys coming?" Pen was waiting in the doorway, her smile trained on Axie. She was trying to make her feel comfortable, to include her.

And that was the only reason Axie relented, following Jace and his family down a long hallway into a dimly lit room. Tears sprung to her eyes, happy ones, for him. She knew how lonely he must have been growing up, because *she'd* been lonely. She missed her mother, every day. And if she was being honest, she missed her father too, the man he was before her mom died. But Jace had found a new family, a chosen family. People who loved him, valued him. People who wanted to share their life with him, and it was the sweetest thing she'd ever witnessed.

And everything she'd ever wanted for herself.

Jace and Baze flanked Pen, crowded the poor sonogram tech. But the woman was smart enough not to ask them to move. Axie stood off to the side, trying to stay out of the way, trying to be as unobtrusive as she could. She watched as the lady squirted gel on Pen's stomach, asking her questions and entering dates into the computer. Then she picked up a wand, pressing it into Pen's belly hard enough to make it kind of dent in.

Then they all looked up at the large screen mounted high on the cream-colored wall. There it was: a tiny blob of a baby, its heartbeat filling the room as it kind of squirmed around. Pen let out an audible breath, like she'd been holding it in this whole time, tears filling her eyes. Baze kissed her hand, the one he was holding between both of his. Jace leaned down, kissing the top of her head. Axie had noticed today that Jace touched Pen easily, without any protest from her mate. She made a mental note to ask why that was okay when Jace wasn't okay with her even being in the same room with any other shifters half the time.

Axie looked up at Jace when he reached back, taking her hand in his. Their eyes met, and she couldn't hide the tears that she'd been wiping from her face since they'd stepped into the room. His gaze narrowed in concern and she shook her head slightly, trying to tell him not to worry about her right now.

"Okay, I'm going to print these first images of your baby and then the doctor will be right in." The lady in the pink scrubs clicked her mouse about a hundred times, and a long scroll of black-and-white pictures started to print. Ten tiny squares of the blob baby.

The tech left the room, closing the door softly behind her, and Baze helped Pen sit up. "You feel better now? We told you he was fine, and you didn't believe us. We'd never lie to you, baby."

Pen dabbed at her eyes, laughing lightly. "I needed to see him. I needed to hear what you guys can hear."

"I went online the other day and ordered you one of those Doppler things." Jace rubbed his hand on her back. "You're right, it's not fair that we can hear him all the time and you can't."

"You can hear the baby's heartbeat?" Axie didn't mean to ask that out loud. Up until that moment she'd kept all questions to herself. But she was sort of amazed that their hearing was that good. She was equally exasperated that she literally knew nothing about shifters. About her own culture. "Is everyone's hearing that sensitive?"

Baze shook his head. "It's easier to pick up on the little things, like the baby's heartbeat, because we're so in synch with Pen. It comes with the mate shar—"

"We're going to go back to waiting room." Jace cut off whatever Baze had been trying to explain. "We'll go get lunch when you're through?" He didn't wait for an answer, squeezing Axie's hand before pulling her out of the room and back down the hallway.

"What was Baze saying? Mate what?" Axie's brain was literally spinning with all the things she didn't know or understand. If her mother were still alive, she would have taught her. Axie was clueless because her father didn't care enough. Maybe she could sit in on one of Pen's classes at St. Leasing. She could hide her hair under a ballcap and her breasts inside one of Jace's oversize sweatshirts.

She wanted to laugh at the image in her mind, her sitting in a classroom full of unbonded shifters while Jace's brain exploded all over the place.

Jace picked a small loveseat this time, basically making her sit on her lap. His arm was resting along the back of the fake leather bench. Fuck. He smelled really good today, spicy and earthy. She took a deep inhale, but all that did was make her want to bury her nose inside his shirt and huff him like a can of spray paint.

"Baze is the pack alpha, and I'm our beta." He was speaking low, and close to her ear so only she could hear his words. Linc had called Jace beta at the meeting, which now made sense. She'd thought it was an odd nickname. "When one is bonded and one isn't, alphas and betas mate share."

Oh wow. "So, like, is sharing a shifter thing I wasn't aware of? Because Rye and Jasper are into sharing and now you and Baze with Pen." Was she supposed to enter some kind of orgy situation? Axie was down to try most things at least once, but she wasn't sure how Jace's shifter would handle that.

"What? No. It's not the same." Jace snorted and Axie was shocked that he was finding any humor in what they were

144

discussing. "Mate sharing isn't sexual. At. All. It's a protective thing, like all my instincts needed to go somewhere, so they transferred to Pen. I care about her, but more like a sister, I guess."

Axie had been right in her assessment earlier. They were family.

A real family.

"So you don't want me to fuck Baz—"

Jace's snarl cut off her joke as he buried his face in her neck, clamping down lightly on her tender flesh. "Are you trying to make me lose control, Axie?"

She shook her head but couldn't seem to form words. Her heart rate sped up, her spine tingling as she started to heat from the inside, her fingers dug into Jace's thigh. Holy shit. She rested her forehead against his chest, trying like hell to calm herself. She pulled him even closer, when she meant to push him away.

"Jace." She panted his name, need evident in her voice.

"Axie?" He put his hands on her shoulders, moving her back so he could see her face. His pupils dilated, his breath hitching in his chest like he was holding it in. "Fuck, come on." He helped her stand, both of them stumbling together into the thankfully empty hallway. Jace hit the button for the elevator, over and over in rapid succession. "Hold on, okay, I just, I need to get us to the car."

There was a ding and then the shiny metal doors opened. The universe was on their side today, because the elevator was all theirs too. Axie stepped away from Jace, his body heat making everything worse. She leaned against the opposite wall, trying like hell to get herself under control. She felt like she was about to hyperventilate. This was worse than last night, so much worse.

There was no denying that what was happening to her wasn't normal.

She licked her lips and Jace groaned, tugging desperately at his own hair. "Please don't do that."

The elevator settled to the bottom floor with a jolt and they darted out into the lobby at the same time. They looked at each other, and then ran toward the outside doors, pushing them wide open. She knew people were staring, but they needed to get to Jace's car. This was Haxton. What if there were other shifters in the area. Jace almost killing his brother was one thing, but a stranger?

That would be a shit show.

Jace hit the remote start button for his SUV as soon as it came into sight, opening the back door for Axie and then all but shoving her inside before climbing in after her. He sat in one of the two bucket seats, hauling her into his lap and fusing his mouth to hers. It was like the culmination of the last three minutes erupted into their kiss. Axie felt wild, frenzied, completely out of control.

They devoured each other, his hands sliding under her dress and her fingers pulling at his hair.

"Fuck, baby." He growled, nipping at her lower jaw. "You've got to try to calm down. This can't happen right now. Not like this."

Not like this? Axie was so turned on, so completely undone by the feel of Jace's hands on her body, she felt high, like her brain and her body were on another plane altogether. If he wanted to slip inside her, if he wanted to claim her in the backseat of his car, she'd let him. Fuck, would she let him.

Jace squeezed her ass, dragging her core against his hard length. "Take deep breaths, baby, please."

"*Me?*" She was panting, riding him relentlessly. "You're not helping things." His every touch sent pleasure coursing through her overheated body. She leaned her head against the seat behind her, exposing her throat and moaning when he sucked at her flesh. "I'm so fucking hot."

Jace reached one hand up, adjusting all the ceiling vents until they were blowing on them. "Better?"

"No." She kissed his mouth as he toyed with her clit through her panties. "Please..." She needed to come, and she needed to be placed inside a damn walk-in freezer. "I need, fuck, I feel like I'm going to explode."

"It's okay, I got you." Jace's hands gripped her hips, guiding her until she was on her knees as he expertly moved her panties to the side. He slipped two fingers inside her pussy, pumping in and out roughly. She let out a loud moan pretty sure that anyone walking by could hear how good Jace was making her feel.

"Baby, come fast, and then you've got to calm the hell down."

"You're making it worse." She covered his lips with hers again, needing him to stop talking. "You're using that commanding tone and you're calling me baby, and it's making me want to combust." Jace let out an entirely smug male chuckle as he used his thumb to press on her clit.

"Don't stop, please, Jace, please don't stop."

She threw her head back, coming the second his teeth attached to her throat. The mixture of pleasure and pain, his possessiveness was all too much and it made stars dance before her closed eyes as her pussy clenched around his fingers.

They were both breathing heavy, their foreheads resting together, trying to regain their control.

"Holy shit." She laughed, turning her face up toward the vent blowing icy air into the car. "That was—"

"Close." Jace roughly squeezed her thighs. "That was really fucking close, Axie."

She was going to go with crazy, or fun. Or crazy fun, because she didn't think she'd ever come so hard before. But the warning in Jace's tone made her open her eyes to meet his gaze, finally noticing how his jaw was once again grinding, his pupils completely blown. "I'm sorry." She put her palm on his chest, feeling his pounding heart. "Are you okay?"

He nodded, closing his eyes for a moment. "When that happens, when you get like that, it's so hard to fight him. To fight for control of the situation. I wanted to tear off your clothes. I wanted slip inside you. I wanted to claim you." He swallowed, running his hands down his face before putting them back on her thighs. "The only reason I was able to hold him off was because you aren't ready."

Jace was right. She wasn't entirely ready to be claimed by him, no matter how much her body would beg to differ. But every minute they spent together, every time he was kind, every time he opened up, hell, every time he turned her on or kissed her throat, she was getting closer.

Axie was starting to like Jace, and *crave* his shifter.

He thought of them as separate beings, but she pictured them as two parts of a whole.

And she was falling for them both.

Chapter Twenty-Nine
Jace

Jace spent the last few hours poring over the dossiers Mathias had recovered for him. Franklin was meticulous about the dirt he had on people, the notes he took. And every file was worse than the next. Jace grew up understanding that there was evil in the world. Hell, he'd met most of these men at one point or another. But reading it in black and white, all the bad they'd done, it was enough to make him sick to his stomach.

"Hey, you ready for us yet?" Jasper came into his office with Riley right behind him, and handed Jace a cold beer.

Baze stretched from where he'd been sitting, his feet propped on Jace's desk and a laptop balanced on his thighs. They had a system going. Jace would read the file, and if he thought maybe it was worth looking into further, he sent it to Baze. So that way, they both knew what they were dealing with.

"Where are the girls?" Riley sat on the floor, his back against the wall. "We came in from a run and didn't see them downstairs."

"Axie is napping with Pen." Jace took a long sip, thankful for the interruption.

"With Pen? Why?" Jasper took the one open chair, extending his long legs out in front of him.

It was safer that way. That was why. Jace knew that if Axie were upstairs in her bed alone, he wouldn't have been able to concentrate. He was still hard from what happened between them in the car that afternoon. Axie's hands had gone to his belt as she climbed off the seat to kneel before him. But he'd stopped her, because he didn't trust himself. He was afraid that once she touched him like that, there would be no controlling his reaction.

Whether she was ready for him or not.

"Pen's hot all the time, she has like three extra fans in there." Baze shut his computer, throwing out an excuse to save Jace from having to answer. "We figured it would help keep Axie, uh, cool."

Riley's eyes widened. "Did she have another episode?"

Jace nodded, trying to push past the lust the memory stirred inside him. "Yeah, but we handled it."

"Handled it?" Jasper grinned, wolfishly. "Or, like, *handled it*."

"One of these days, he's going to rip out your constantly wagging tongue." Baze shook his head, like he was beyond baffled. "And none of us are going to blame him."

Jasper waved away Baze's concern, chuckling lightly. "I'm comic relief, and without me you'd all die of boredom."

"What's the plan? Did you find anything in the stuff Mathias sent over?" Riley deftly changed the subject, reading the room and knowing that Jace wasn't in the mood to joke about what was happening between him and Axie.

Jace stood, twirling his pen between his fingers, feeling a little stiff and restless. He needed to go for a run too, but he wasn't comfortable leaving Axie alone in the house.

"I read it all, everything Franklin had on the men who worked with him and for him." Jace had read for so long his eyes hurt. "They're the worst. Every single one of them."

"But you knew that, right?" Jasper, thankfully, seemed to be ready to put on his big-boy pants and adult for the time being. "You grew up surrounded by this shit. Franklin was grooming you to take over."

"He was." Jace tossed his pen down onto his glass desk. "But here's the deal. Franklin, from what he shared with me, was a man who dealt in information. He greased politicians and kept state officials in his suit pocket. Strong-armed mergers and made acquisitions. He'd buy whole corporations, then dismantle them and sell them for parts. He hoarded secrets. He did favors. Say someone wanted to open a casino but was having trouble getting their liquor license. Franklin would step in and fix it."

"He was the godfather," Riley spoke up from his spot on the rug.

"I don't know a lot about what Franklin did before he was in charge, all that happened before I was old enough to know better." Which was probably a good thing. Watching his father murder and maim his way to the top would have probably fucked him up even more. "So yeah, for as long as I can remember, he was the boss. The godfather, if we're using Hollywood references here."

Baze snorted out an annoyed laugh. "He's been hanging out with Corey too long. She relates everything to a movie she's seen."

"Getting to the top is messy, but once you're up there, your hands stay relatively clean. Which is how he got away with so much for so long." Jace tapped his finger on Baze's closed laptop. "These men, the ones he had information on, they did the dirty work. He simply helped them and then held it over their heads until he needed a favor."

"Like Lucifer." Riley nodded, as if he completely understood.

Jasper rolled his eyes when Jace and Baze both looked confused. "It's a TV show. Ignore him." He stood, stepping closer to Jace's desk. "So who do we go after? Who do we need to convince that we don't want our father's throne? Is it Axie's father?"

Jace couldn't help his bark of laughter. "That pissant? No way. He's a suit. A crooked lawyer, men like him are a dime a dozen in Franklin's world. He didn't even have the spine to come to us on his own, he tried to pimp out his daughter." For which he'd be punished, eventually. "In my experience the man who has the biggest balls is the top contender."

"The guy who attacked Ax?" Riley took Jasper's vacated chair. "He's our guy?"

"No, but I bet he works for our guy." Jace knew he was right, because this was the shit his father had taught him. These were his bedtime stories, his dinner table discussions. Franklin had wanted Jace to work beside him, and then take over when he was dead and gone. But Jace had never wanted that life, never wanted to be under his father's control. "We get the dipshit doing his bidding, and we use him to find out who is really in charge."

"Then what?" Jasper asked the question, but everyone seemed to be holding their breath waiting for the answer.

That was the part Jace hadn't figured out yet. After reading about the men who would take Franklin's place, he wasn't so sure what he should do. They were evil, vile. So how did he, in good conscience, hand one of them that kind of power? The kind of power Franklin had, the kind he abused.

"One step at a time." Baze finally sat back down. "How do we lure this guy out?"

"Bait." Jace collapsed back in his leather office chair. "Riley, you're taking Axie out on a date."

Jasper's jaw dropped open. "Are you serious?"

"We'll all be close. Riley will wear a wire and an earpiece." Jace had been thinking about this exact thing when Jasper and Riley had walked in a few minutes ago. "You two eat, laugh, and act oblivious to your surroundings." Jasper would have been better at this little acting gig, but Jace would be damned if he would let Axie be alone with him. Riley he trusted, for the most part. "Don't fucking touch her though." He stood pointing at his friend. "If I see you touch her, I swear I will lose my shit."

"I get it." Riley held his hands up. "Make her laugh, don't make her come."

Jace clamped his jaws shut, his molars grinding at Riley's rare attempt at pissing him off.

Baze threw his arm out across Jace's chest, like he'd been prepared to have to hold him back. "You two get out of here, go get dressed, and stop fucking with your brother."

Your brother.

After Jasper and Riley left his office, laughing down the hallway, Baze closed the door. "You are, you know? Their brother, Jasper's by blood and Riley's by pack. You're my beta. You're closer to me than anyone other than Pen. And my mate? Fuck does she love you something fierce."

Baze's softly spoken words were making emotions build in Jace's chest.

"We're having a baby, you, me, and Pen. The three of us prayed for that baby, wished for him. I know it hurt you as much as it hurt me when she'd cry every month she wasn't pregnant. You held her almost as often as I did." Jace wiped at his eyes, refusing to look at his alpha. "And now, there's Axie."

"I never wanted, I never thought, uh…" Jace wasn't sure how to put into words the way he felt about Axie, the way he felt about what was growing between them.

"It's not your fault, kid." Baze put his hand on Jace's shoulder. "You never wanted a mate. You were taught they were a weakness. And when you saw us all fall in love, you realized Franklin was wrong. But by that point you were convinced that you didn't deserve a love like that. That you'd hit your quota of happiness and any more would throw the universe off balance."

"I'm not a good guy."

"You were raised by a bad man, and he demanded terrible things from a child. But you, you put everyone's safety above your own. You put up with your dickwad of a twin, and you work to protect Riley's soft heart. You shower Pen with affection and friendship." Baze shook him lightly. "That's what I'm trying to tell you, kid, you're one of the best men I've ever known, and you deserve as much happiness as your surly ass can handle."

Jace didn't think he could handle much more of his packmates telling him how great he was. Maybe one day, he'd be able to believe them.

Jace wasn't sure what to say and he was almost afraid that his voice would crack if he even tried to speak. Instead he threw his arms around Baze, initiating a hug for probably the first time in his life.

Chapter Thirty
Axie

Axie knocked on Jace's office door before pushing it open to find him and Baze hugging, like father and son. For the second time that day, she started to cry. It had to be all the crazy shit wreaking havoc on her body, like the hot flashes.

Both of them pulled apart, Baze smiling and Jace with his eyes trained on the top of his desk. He didn't like showing emotion. It seemed to make him feel ashamed. She understood that. Her father didn't put up with that kind of stuff either. After her mother passed away, she'd learned real quick to never let her sadness show.

"Sorry, I didn't mean to interrupt. Rye said you needed to see me." She'd run into him in the kitchen. She'd woken up starving after her nap. They'd never had a chance to go to lunch after Pen's appointment. Jace had been too concerned that she'd have another episode.

"You didn't." Baze held his arm out, gesturing her inside the room. "I'm going to go check on Pen. Jace, you can go over tonight's plan with Axie?" He posed it like a question, like he wasn't altogether sure that Jace was capable of telling her what was up. But Jace nodded, still not looking at either one of them. "And, kid, you need to um, well, you need to spend some time with Axie before we leave, you feel me?"

At that question, Jace picked his head up. "Yeah, I get it."

Baze shut the door, leaving them alone for the first time since what had gone down in the car.

"You guys are talking in code again." Axie hopped on Jace's desk, her legs swinging.

He sat down in a tall-backed leather rolling chair. "It wasn't code. He didn't want to make you uncomfortable." He grabbed her legs, pulling himself closer to her. "I need you to go out to dinner with Riley tonight and be bait."

She raised her brows in surprise. "Really? Because that seems like something your wolf would have a real big problem with."

"He does. He's beyond fucking pissed at this plan." Jace rubbed his palms on her thighs, the shorts she'd changed back into from breakfast leaving them bare and exposed. "But I need to try to draw out the man who attacked you the other night. I have to eliminate that threat and find out who he is working for. I'll be close the whole time. So will Jasper and Baze. And I trust Riley. You're safe with him."

"If this is what you need me to do, then I'm game." She'd do anything he asked of her at this point, not only because she sought redemption, but because she wanted to make him happy. She wanted to make him proud, and she wanted to contribute to his pack. "But, uh, what happens if my body spazzes out in the middle of this dinner stakeout?" She gripped the edge of his desk, shrugging her shoulders. "I don't have any control over it."

"No, but *I* can manipulate it a bit." His hands shot out, taking hold of her hips and bringing her into his lap. "That's what Baze was talking about before he left."

Axie rested her arms on his shoulders, a tad shocked that he was being so bold. He touched her the first night she was here, only to kiss her pain away. The second night, he'd taken things further, but he told her he wasn't the one in control. Today in the car, that was strictly need based, neither one of them had a choice. But this right now, the way he was holding her, searching her face, it felt different somehow.

"Manipulate it?" She ran her fingers through his dark hair, smiling to herself when he closed his eyes as if he was enjoying it. "How?"

His jaw started to clench at her last question, like it always did when he was thinking too hard.

Or fighting his shifter side.

"You need to go upstairs and get dressed. Lock the door, don't open it until I come for you." He leaned forward, resting his head on her chest, his breaths coming out in short bursts. "I have to do it right before we leave the house."

"Do what?" She hugged her arms around his neck, still not entirely sure what he was trying to tell her. "I don't know your codes, beta."

He pulled away from her, then picked her up and put her back on her feet. "I don't feel in control right now, baby. I need you to go."

Baby.

Every time he called her that, her core tightened. She had such a visceral reaction to his words, even the different tones he used when he spoke had the ability to send her teetering close to the edge.

She held out her hand, palm up. "Give me your phone."

"Why?" His gaze narrowed at her demand. "What do you need it for?"

She smiled, wicked and flirty. "I feel a hot flash coming on. I need the air upstairs to be blasting."

A low growl started in his throat, making her laugh lightly. "I'll fix the AC, just go." He pointed toward his door with one hand and gently pushed her in that direction with the other. "I mean it, Axie."

She bit at her lower lip as she walked out of his office backward so she could toy with him for a few more seconds. She liked this version of Jace, possessive but soft. It was the perfect combination, not that Axie had ever spent much time contemplating what she would want out of a mate one day.

Axie honestly assumed that she would float through the rest of her life unattached and completely free. And that was the way she wanted it. At least, that was what she thought she wanted, until she met Jace. It'd only been a few days, but she couldn't imagine an existence without him.

Riley was in the living room, sprawled out on the couch, as Axie walked past on her way to the stairs. She stopped, crossing her arms over her chest. "Well?"

"Well what?" His forehead wrinkled in confusion.

"Are you going to ask me out? For our date?"

Riley sat up further, looking toward the hallway. "Where's Jace?"

"Stewing in his office." Axie jerked her thumb back in the direction she'd come.

"You can't play with him on this." Riley shook his head, his tone serous. "It's already hard enough on him."

Axie scoffed, waving away Riley's apparent concern. "Jace needs *more* play in his life, not less."

"Yes. That's what I've been trying to tell you guys." Jasper stepped off the last step, holding his hand up, requesting a high five. "Good girl, make him have some fucking fun every once in a while." She slapped his palm, laughing in agreement.

"Axie." All eyes flew to the no-longer-empty hallway to see Jace standing there in that power stance of his. "Now."

"Okay, okay, geez." She started up the stairs, calling over her shoulder on the way up. "But you better hurry and get up here, I think I figured out what your code talk was about, and I'm getting hotter by the second."

Jasper's laughter couldn't drown out Jace's growl that seemed to shake the house.

Chapter Thirty-One
Jace

Jace tried the knob on Axie's bedroom door, groaning in frustration when he found it unsecured. He threw it open and then slammed it closed behind him, throwing the lock into place as loudly as he possibly could. "Dammit, Axie, what did I tell you?"

He stopped short, his rant dying before it could fully form.

Axie was lying on her bed, naked, with two extra fans pointed directly at her body.

"I was joking earlier, about feeling the hot flash, but then the second I got done doing my hair, it hit. I managed to run into Pen's room and steal her fans, but I guess I forget to lock the door." She was waving her hands in front of her face, taking any added breeze she could get. "Sorry."

She was lying in here, spread out and exposed, with the door unlocked. What would have happened if Jasper had walked by? Jace wanted to be angry that she'd put herself in danger like that, but she looked so comically miserable.

"Next time, text me." He crossed the room to stand at the foot of the bed. "I could have gotten the fans, I could have made sure that everyone stayed downstairs." And by everyone, he meant his twin.

Axie propped herself up on her elbows. "My brain stops working when the hot flashes hit." She pursed her lips, glancing down her body. "It's the second time today, it's happening more often."

He nodded, letting his eyes get his fill of her completely bare before him for the first time. "That's how it works. There will be less and less time between episodes. It's your body losing patience."

"You said you could *manipulate* it, right?" She fell back against her pillows again, like she was as frustrated as she was uncomfortable.

"Yeah, baby, I can." He reached out, grabbing one of her ankles and making her yelp as he dragged her closer to him.

"You or your shifter?" Her voice was shaky. "Who am I dealing with here?"

"Me." Jace chuckled quietly. "If you were dealing with my shifter, what's about to happen in here would end differently."

"Well, then you best get to manipulating because I feel like I am about to catch on fire." She fanned her face again, the movement making her breasts bounce enticingly.

Jace crawled up her body, kissing her neck, breathing in the fresh scent of her perfume. He let his teeth graze her throat, not liking that she'd covered up his mark. He moved farther down, sucking and nipping at her collarbone, claiming her in the only way he could right now.

"Your wolf needs to quit, my dress is low cut." Her words came out all breathy, not much threat behind them.

He smiled against her skin, biting her again. "Wear something else."

Her hands went to his hair, tugging him away from her chest and playfully pushing him farther down her body. "Make me come, I have a date to go on."

His shifter wasn't a fan of her joke, but Jace thought it was so funny he couldn't help but laugh. Axie made him feel lighter. Maybe she was right, he needed more of this in his life. "Okay, baby."

She moaned, either from him calling her baby or what he started doing to her afterward, he wasn't sure.

***

Jace and Axie walked down the stairs, hand in hand. She was no longer feeling overheated, but he sure as hell was. After he'd made her come, once with his fingers and once more with his tongue for good measure, she tried again to return the favor. But he was too afraid of what would happen if he got that worked up. She wasn't ready.

Jasper, Riley, and Baze were waiting for them in the living room. Baze had taken Pen into town earlier to stay at Keller and Molly's until they were done trying to trap Axie's attacker.

"Well, don't you look beautiful, all dressed up for a date with a shifter who isn't your mate." Jasper winked at her, earning a strong flick in the forehead from Jace.

"Thanks." Axie frowned down at the little black dress that fit her like a glove. "I was going to wear something else, but Jace's wolf lost his shit and marked up my, um, chest."

Jace glared at Jasper, then Riley, telling them without words that he wasn't in the mood for any more of their crap. He was about to send Axie out as bait, and he was feeling way on edge: totally restless and itching for a fight. He wanted to destroy the man who hurt her, almost as much as he wanted to shove her against the nearest wall and bury his perpetually hard dick inside her tight pussy.

"Hello? Earth to Jace?"

Riley waved his hand in front of his face, snapping him out of his violent and sexual thoughts. "Huh?"

"They asked if you were ready to go." Axie slipped her hand in his, pulling him toward the front door. "Are you okay?"

"Yeah, I am." He led her down the front steps to the car she and Riley were going to take. "You're going to ride into town with Riley, but we'll be close behind you." Jace opened her car door, stepping into her space before she had a chance to get inside. "If you start to feel bad, or weird, or *anything*, you tell Riley immediately. You understand?"

She nodded.

He grabbed her chin, bringing her lips to his for a lingering kiss, ignoring all the gasps of surprise from his so-called family standing in the driveway.

"Holy shit. Did Jace just kiss his girl in front of us? I feel like we need to mark this day on the calendar."

"Leave him alone, Jasper." Baze shoved him into the SUV, slamming the door in his face before he could say anything else.

"I'll take care of her, I promise." Riley knocked on the top of the low sports car before settling inside.

Jace sighed, kissing Axie one more time, then turning his back on her to walk to the other vehicle. He didn't seem able to watch her get in the car with Riley and drive off. It was the separation, and the fact that he was sending her off with an unbonded male. But it was also that he was pretty sure he was starting to more than like her.

Way more.

Chapter Thirty-Two
Axie

Axie was ashamed to admit, even if only to herself, that this was the first date she'd been on in a long time. Fake or not. The restaurant was nice, the lighting dim, a candle in a glass votive flickering on the middle of the table. No one had questioned her age when she'd ordered a bottle of expensive champagne and her meal was delicious.

The only problem was Riley. He was being a little stiff, and a lot boring.

"You need to lighten up, Rye." She picked up her crystal flute, tapping it to his with a grin on her face. "Life is hard enough, you need to enjoy the small moments when you can."

"We're bait for a violent criminal." Riley was leaning forward, whispering across the table.

She sighed, like she felt bad for him. "You're right, and once we get back to the house, we'll be prisoners for Jace's safekeeping. So, why not enjoy this nice meal out." She gestured to the table full of food between them. "We're friends, we're here, why not have fun?"

He deflated slightly, his features softening. "I'm sorry."

"Don't apologize, there's no need." She used the tip of her finger to push his glass of champagne closer to him. "Talk to me, and enjoy this ridiculously expensive bubbly that Jace is going to foot the bill for."

"Speaking of Jace, how are things going with you two?"

She pursed her lips. "He hasn't thrown me out of any vehicles today, so that's promising."

"He cares for you."

"His shifter cares for me. Jace, well, he's getting there, I guess." She shrugged, trying, and most likely failing, to seem unaffected that he might never be ready to claim her.

Riley finally gave in, sipping at his champagne. "You're good for him."

"You think?" She took a bite of her perfectly cooked salmon.

"You play with him, you give him a hard time. You make him laugh even when he tries to hide it. You remind me of Jasper sometimes, except you know when you can push Jace's boundaries and when you need to stand down. Jasper hasn't figured out that delicate balance yet."

She placed her fork down, finally full and laughing. "Oh, I'm sure he has, but he doesn't care."

"You might be right." Riley's smile was so sweet she barely restrained her urge to reach across the table and ruffle his floppy red hair.

"What's the deal with you and Jasper? You really share *everything*?" Axie put emphasis on the last word, wagging her eyebrows for added affect.

"We share *more* than most best friends, and that's all I'm going to tell you while we're sitting in this crowded restaurant. Besides, Jace is hissing in my ear, telling me to stop talking about sex with you."

Axie choked on the sip of champagne she'd taken. "He can hear us?"

"Yes."

She sat her glass down, eyes narrowed. "What else is he saying?"

"He said I can't let you have any more champagne because it's going to make your blood pump faster, and that could trigger a reaction." Riley reached across the table, stealing her flute and draining it dry. "He also didn't love your comment about you being a prisoner in his house. He may have said something about the treatment being better and the conjugal visits much more frequent."

Axie giggled. "Hey, if Jace is making sex jokes, I'll count that as a win."

Chapter Thirty-Three
Jace

Jace watched Axie throw her head back and laugh at whatever story Riley was telling her. She'd been right to make him loosen up. He'd been uptight, on guard. And anyone with a trained eye would have seen their dinner for what it was, a setup.

"That guy still watching them?" Jasper was in the backseat of the heavily tinted SUV, crammed into a ball on the floorboard. That was the seat he'd earned himself after he asked Jace how many times he'd *handled* Axie's problem before he'd let her leave the house.

Jace moved his gaze from the table in front of a large window he'd reserved for her and Riley to the alley across the street. "Yeah, he's still there." There was a man in shadows, a black ball cap pulled low over his head.

"They're paying, about to leave." Baze was watching the restaurant.

They were all quiet as Axie and Riley left the small bistro, walking down the mostly empty street toward the ice cream shop on the corner.

"Damnit." Jace cursed, frustrated and tired of seeing Axie with Riley. "He's watching, but he's not making a move to follow them."

"Of course he's not." Jasper crawled closer to the window, pressing his nose against the dark glass. "They look like two teenagers out on a study date. You had them in a romantic restaurant with candlelight and shit, and now they're strolling down the street like a girl and the guy she put in the friend zone. They need to sell it and you've gotta give them permission to do it."

Was his brother currently high? He wanted Jace to give his friend permission to put his hands on his girl? The girl that was made to be his, the girl he'd yet to fully claim. It would be a cold day in hell. "No."

"He's right, kid," Baze spoke up. "Otherwise we're going to lose him and he'll go report back that something weird is going on, or at the very least that Axie lied and she's closer to you guys than she told him."

"It's not going to happen. Don't fucking push me, either of you." Jace ground his teeth together, trying to calm his annoyance that they were even asking this of him.

"This is fucking ridiculous." Jasper climbed over the seat in a huff. "Baze, restrain Jace."

Jace was so shocked when Baze actually did what Jasper told him that it made him easier to take down. His alpha dove on top of him, wedging him in the floorboard and then holding him in place. "Are you fucking kidding me? Let me go, Baze. I'm about to lose my shit."

"No you won't." Baze added a bit of pressure. "I'm your fucking alpha and I'm telling you to stay the hell down there."

Jace opened his mouth to protest, but no words came out. Holy shit. Baze had never commanded him to do something he didn't want to do. And he was pissed when he realized his wolf was going to listen. His shifter was okay with what Baze was asking of him. This time it was Jace that wasn't. His human side was the one who wanted to fight to get to Axie.

Jasper grabbed the walkie-talkie that had dropped to the floor in the scuffle. "Riley, it's Jasper, can you hear me?" Jasper paused, like he was waiting for a signal. "Okay, good, don't worry about Jace, listen to me and do exactly as I say."

Jace closed his eyes, positive that he was going to end up killing someone before the night was over.

Chapter Thirty-Four
Axie

Axie and Riley were walking down the street, side by side, talking about what classes he was planning to take in the fall. She thought the topic would make her sad or jealous since getting out of Haxton was all she'd dreamed about for the last few years. But she was neither of those things: instead she felt excited for him.

She looked down when he reached out and grabbed her hand. They were supposed to be a couple running around behind Jace's back, so it made sense that they needed to hold hands. She went along with it, and then yelped in surprise when Riley suddenly shoved her against a brick wall, pressing his body against hers, his thigh between her legs.

Axie pushed at his hips, afraid that Jace would kill the poor kid. "Rye, what the hell?"

"They're in my ear, remember?" He was whispering, his fingers threading in her hair to bring her even closer. "There was a guy watching us have dinner, but he wasn't making a move. They need us to try to force his hand."

She nodded, willing her pulse to slow. "Okay. It's okay."

"Tell me if you start to feel, um, well, you know."

"I'm good. Do whatever they're telling you."

He buried his face in her neck, the side that Jace hadn't marked, and she wondered if that was intentional. Riley groaned, not like he was turned on but more like he was annoyed. "He said you better fucking sell it because the guy is making his way toward us."

She let her head fall back as she hiked her thigh up Riley's hip.

"Just like that. Good girl." He grabbed her leg, grinding against her core. "Sorry, that's Jasper, he's talking in my ear."

Jasper? She assumed it was Jace that was giving Riley permission to touch her. If Jace wasn't the one directing them, then was he even okay with any of this?

"He's a few yards away, he's closing in." Riley's lips skimmed her jaw, his hand snaking around to palm her ass through her short dress. "It's okay, Ax. It's all going to be okay."

She whimpered from the panic she was starting to feel crawling up her throat. "Rye, you've got to stop, I can't."

"You can. It's almost over." He was all over her now, his hands roaming.

"You're scaring me."

"No, I'm not." His heavy breaths were in her ear. "Jace is out of the car now, your body is responding to him. When he's around, anyone else's touch feels wrong. Take deep breaths. I promise I will never hurt you." She closed her eyes, trying to follow his instructions. "When I tell you to, duck out of my arms and run to the car. You understand?"

"Yes," she moaned the word, like someone in the throes of passion.

"Ready?" Riley scraped his teeth across her neck. "Now."

Axie did exactly as Riley told her to. She ducked out of his arms and immediately ran to the car. It beeped right before she got to it, and she climbed into the passenger seat and locked the doors. Her heart was racing, out of fear, not excitement.

She felt like she had bugs crawling all over her skin. She'd never experienced anything like it before. *Wrong.* Riley had felt so fucking wrong pressed against her. It took everything she had not to scream, not to try to fight him off.

She turned in her seat in time to see Jace and Baze shove a man dressed in all black into the back of an SUV. She knew from talking with Riley on the ride over that they were going to take the guy to a warehouse on the outskirts of town. And there, they'd make him tell them who he was working for. That was the plan anyway.

When the driver's side door opened, she jumped in surprise. "Rye? Is everything okay?" She'd been hoping that Jace would be the one to drive her home. She wanted to see him, to talk to him. She wanted to make sure that he wasn't mad.

"Uh, yeah, we're all good." He started the car and pulled away from the curb. "Jace is going to go with Baze and Jasper to the warehouse. He'll be home soon."

"What aren't you telling me?" She recognized the hesitation in Riley's tone and the clipped way he was speaking.

"When Jasper was telling me what to, um, do to you, I thought Jace was there. I thought he was watching and directing the whole situation." Riley's hands white-knuckled the steering wheel.

"He wasn't?"

He shook his head. "Baze held him down while Jasper took over."

Axie was worried about him. Baze and Riley were two of the only males he seemed to trust, and one held him down while the other put his hands and mouth all over her body. Jace was always so torn between his human side and his shifter, she wondered which one would win out when it came to her.

"How pissed is he?"

"Let's put it this way." Riley checked his rearview mirror, like he was making sure they weren't being followed. "If Jasper comes back to the house unconscious, we'll count it as a win."

She let her head fall back against her seat, exhaustion weighing on her. Her hot flash episodes wore her out, and the stuff Jace did to her body to make them go away didn't help. She'd already had one nap today, and that was probably the only reason she was able to keep her eyes open as they drove home in comfortable silence.

Axie had protested at first, not wanting to take a nap with a woman she barely knew. Pen was nice, but still, sleeping next to someone you'd only had one conversation with was odd.

"If you don't come in here, he won't do what he needs to downstairs." Pen had opened her door wider, inviting Axie in.

"Um, yeah, okay." She'd given in, knowing that Jace needed to look through all those files and find out who had attacked her.

Pen told Axie about how she and Baze had been apart for ten years. About the events that brought them back together. Axie told her about her mom, how much she missed her, and she talked about her father, about why she wanted to leave Colorado to get away from him. She told Pen about the moment she realized her father was an evil man. He'd come home with blood on one of his crisp white button-downs. She'd asked if he was okay and he'd laughed in her face. The sound so unfamiliar.

Pen filled Axie in on all the things Jace hadn't had the chance or the heart to tell her. About how Jasper grew up safe and loved, and that Franklin had raised Jace by himself. She told Axie about how Jace had tried to protect his twin from their father, and all the ways Franklin had tormented their pack over the last couple of years. She said that was why Jace was so protective, and that he thought it was all his fault.

But it wasn't. And no one blamed him.

They loved him, they all did. And Pen said she hoped that one day, Axie could love him too.

Axie had closed her eyes, a tear escaping, as she whispered that she already did.

Chapter Thirty-Five
Jace

Baze and Jasper kept silent on the drive to the warehouse, the way Jace had instructed them to. He didn't want the prisoner they had tied up in the back to hear anything that he could use against them. It took all the strength Jace had left to keep his mouth shut, to keep from tearing his twin a brand-new asshole.

And Baze too, for that matter.

The two of them had held him down, refusing to let him watch Axie and Riley against the goddamn brick wall. But he could hear it all, Jasper's instructions, Riley's whispered words to Axie, her soft pants and moans. When they'd finally let him up, he'd stepped out of the car in time to see Riley bite her neck. In that moment, he forgot about the reason they were all there, the reason his best friend's hands were on his girl. If Axie hadn't ducked and run, Jace would have gone after Riley instead of the man stalking him.

Seeing the look of disgust on her face was the only thing that saved any of them.

"Stop, you're doing that wrong." Baze swatted Jasper's hands out of the way and took over cuffing their newest prisoner to the chain hanging from the ceiling. "His toes need to touch or his shoulder will dislocate too quickly."

"Can you two not correct each other in front of that asshole?" Jace shook his head. "He's out now, but he could come to at any moment."

When they'd brought him into the warehouse, Jace had unleashed some of his pent-up anger and aggression on the guy. Not only was he paying him back for what he'd done to Axie when he'd attacked her, but he was also exercising the rage he had for Baze and Jasper. And Riley. After the guy passed out, Jace kept going until the asshole was covered in blood, and it took his alpha and his twin to pull him off.

They'd made him go into the next room and clean up.

"You need to go home." Baze shook his head, pointing to the door. "Your head is too messed up for you to be here, and you know it."

Jace was the one who taught Baze everything he knew about torture tactics. Like the fact that if your brain wasn't focused solely on the task at hand, you'd never get the information you were after. Baze spitting Jace's lessons back at him was pissing him off.

"I'm fine."

Jasper snorted. "Like fuck."

Jace ignored him, speaking only to his alpha. "We need a name before this gets any more out of hand." He glanced at the man hanging from the ceiling. "Miguel Contreau, and whoever this guy works for? They're two men in a group of dozens. We don't have time to waste."

"You beat the shit out of him." Jasper grabbed the man by the hair, pulling his swollen face up and then letting it drop. "He's a shifter in a healing sleep, you aren't getting any information out of him until tomorrow."

"I hate agreeing with him, you know that." Baze sighed. "But Jasper is right."

"Look, go home to your girl like we all know you're dying to do." Jasper flipped off the dim lights on the large space, opening the door to the adjoining room they used to keep supplies and to clean up. "I'll drop Baze at my apartment. He and Pen can stay there tonight. I need to go check on Maddi and the baby, as much as that pains me to say. So you and Ax can have the house to yourselves."

Jace reluctantly followed him and Baze out of the building. "The house to ourselves? Riley's there."

"Don't you worry about Riley." Jasper sent him a toothless grin. "He likes to watch."

Jace pulled back, fully prepared to knock out his brother, but Baze got there first.

"Ow, coach, I think you broke my nose." Jasper's voice was muffled, his hands cupping his face as blood flowed to the ground.

"He's had a shit night, and I told you earlier to stop messing with him." Baze opened the car door, grabbing a discarded shirt for Jasper to use to stay the bleeding. "You're lucky I beat him to it, because we both know he would have laid you out."

"His night would have been a lot shittier if I hadn't taken over back there." Jasper took the rag Baze offered him, pressing it to his nose as he leaned his head back.

"Are you insane?" Jace hit Jasper's elbow, making him jostle his nose. "You had Baze hold me down while you instructed your best friend how and where to touch my mate." He screamed those last words, the sound echoing around the metal building.

"And I did it for you, you asswipe." Jasper moved out of the way when Jace went to knock his arm again. "What would have happened if that guy hadn't taken the bait? Huh? You would've blamed yourself. You would have internalized all that shit."

"He has a point, kid." Baze shrugged one shoulder. "I didn't enjoy giving you an order like that, but it was the right call."

"I *know* you, Jace, we're fucking twins." Jasper pulled the rag away from his nose, and then put it right back when the blood kept coming. "I know when to push you. I know how much you can take. You guys think I'm an idiot skating through life on my good looks and how well I swing a bat. But I'm not stupid."

Jace smiled despite himself. "You're sorta stupid, but I agree. You're not an idiot."

"Come on, you two, let's get out of here." Baze shoved them both toward the car.

Jace opened the driver's-side door. "I'll drop you guys off where you need to go, but I think I'm going to head back to town. I want to check the area, see if anyone is looking for our friend back there."

"No, I'll do it on my way to Linc and Maddi's." Jasper had his head leaned back, the shirt still pressed to his face. "You need to go home."

"I can't go home. I'm afraid to see her." Jace hadn't meant to be so honest. It'd slipped out without his permission. But now seemed as good a time as any to try the whole letting people in thing.

Baze turned in his seat. "Why?"

There was no use in trying to lie now that he'd already shared too much anyway. "It's getting harder and harder to control my wolf, and I'm worried that when I see her, I'll remember the way she looked in Riley's arms."

"And that you won't be able to stop yourself?" Baze finished for him.

He nodded, not taking his eyes off the road.

"You won't do anything she doesn't want." Baze put his hand on Jace's shoulder in a fatherly gesture that he'd never experienced growing up with Franklin. "You know that."

"That's what I'm scared of, that she's ready."

Axie understood what was happening, the road they were headed down. But in Jace's eyes, it was still all his fault. He was the shifter. He was the one who could truly bond them together. Her body was betraying her, not taking into consideration what she really wanted.

She was nothing like him. She was wild. She yearned to be free. She liked to laugh and dance, she relished every chance she got to lose control. Before her father had shoved her in Jace's path, she'd planned to leave Colorado. She had a life she loved all mapped out. But if he claimed her, she was stuck with him forever. He could never leave his pack, and he'd never survive without Axie by his side.

"I'm going to ruin her life." Jace gripped the steering wheel, the sound of his hands on the leather loud in the quiet car. "Axie isn't anything like me. I'll stifle her. She'll be like a caged bird."

"The problem with you, bro, is that you don't see yourself the way the rest of us see you." Jasper was talking with the rag still pressed against his nose, making his serious words sound a little comical. "You give every single one of us the freedom to be ourselves. We all skip and frolic through life, fucking and laughing without a care in the goddamn world. And do you know why? Because we know that you're there in the background, making sure that we're all safe." He put his free hand on the back of Jace's seat. "As far as Axie goes, you're right, she's a wild one. She likes a good time, and she loves a brief escape from reality. So fucking give it to her. No one will ever be able to blow her mind like you can. Hell, it's what you were born to do."

Chapter Thirty-Six

Axie

The first thing she did when she got home was run upstairs and take a long shower. Not too hot. She didn't want to trigger another event. Riley basically demanded it of her. He said that if Jace came home and she smelled like another shifter, he'd beat the crap out of said shifter.

When she got out, she'd thrown on one of Jace's shirts he'd left in her room for good measure. The last thing she wanted was for Jace to beat up on Riley, who was probably the kindest male on the face of the planet. Which was reinforced when he was sitting next to her on the couch with a nice fire going in the fireplace, while they waited up for everyone.

She knew Jace would have preferred her locked in her room, but she felt shaky and she didn't want to be alone. Riley was putting his neck on the line for her, again.

"You're right, this show is really good."

He nodded. "I know. Corey and I binged it in like two weekends." He clicked the pause button, the screen stopping on a yummy and shirtless Tom Ellis. "How you doing? The whiskey helping?"

Riley had poured her a glass of whiskey from Jace's bar cart, telling her it would calm her nerves, like she didn't already know that all too well. "Expensive booze soothes my soul." She rested her head on his arm, feeling more and more like her old self every minute. "Tell me about that adorable baby you're obsessed with."

"Hadley." He lit up at the mention of her. "I'm her cosmic guardian. I sort of fell in love with her the second she came into existence. That's why Corey and I are so close."

"And Jasper? He's linked to Maddi and Linc's baby girl?"

Riley nodded.

No one had told her anything, but she'd picked up things here and there from conversations she'd overheard in the house when people thought she wasn't listening. It was a skill she'd learned from a young age. She knew it was something Jace and she had in common from their childhoods. He refused to acknowledge their similarities, choosing to focus on their differences instead.

"We're all alone here, no Jace in your ear." Axie gave him a wicked smile. "You ready to tell me what's really going on with you and Jasper?"

"Nope."

"What? Why not? I can keep a secret."

Riley got to his feet. "Number one, you know exactly what's going on. You want to hear the dirty details because you are a bad girl." He glanced at his cell. "Two, Jace is pulling into the driveway and I need to be out of sight when he comes inside." He leaned down and placed a soft kiss to the top of her head. "Ax, do you want him? Do you want to be his?"

Axie had never thought much about belonging to, or rather being with, anyone. After her mother passed and her father became unrecognizable, her life became about survival. And then straight up fucking defiance, which led to her simply wanting to get away.

Going to college out of state was all she'd thought about since her first day of high school. But since she'd been here with Jace, she'd barely thought about it at all. If she chose Jace, if she chose their bond, she'd be living in Haxton, Colorado, for the foreseeable future.

But she'd be *here*.

She'd be hanging out with Riley, laughing with Jasper, talking with Pen.

She'd be with Jace, always.

Axie smiled, in love with the truth behind her answer. "Yes."

Riley shrugged one shoulder, his grin going a little wicked. "If you want him to claim you, you're going to have to push him."

"How?" She narrowed her eyes, not sure what he was getting at.

"Speak to his shifter."

Riley walked out of the room, and she watched as he made his way up the stairs. He really seemed to enjoy throwing out truth bombs and then ghosting. His bedroom door closed the same moment the front door opened. Jace came inside, tossing his keys on the table in the entryway. He ran his hands through his hair, sighing as he stepped into the living room. She wasn't sure he even realized she was standing there watching his every move.

She cleared her throat. "You're home."

His head shot up, his eyes meeting hers across the room. He stopped where he stood, taking a deep breath.

"Did you get the information you needed? A name?" She bit at her bottom lip, not trying to rile him up but out of nervousness.

Jace shook his head. "He passed out pretty quick. We're going to try in the morning." He took one small step toward her. "Are you okay? I saw how upset you were, and I'm sorry. Jasper should have never made Riley do that. We could have found another way."

"I'm made of stronger stuff than that."

He nodded, then turned to the stairs. Was he going to want to go to bed? Axie's skin started to heat, the tingle building at the base of her spine. If they went up there, what would happen? Would he want to wait another day? Would he make her come, and then nip her skin until she fell asleep? She didn't want that, not again. She wanted more.

She wanted to belong to him.

Riley's suggestion played like a loop in her brain: *speak to his shifter.*

"But yeah, it felt wrong." She put her hand on her neck, the side Riley had buried his face in. "Rye, his touch, his teeth…"

"What are you doing, Axie?"

"You asked if I was okay." He was standing still again, so she took a few steps toward him. "I am now, but I wasn't, you know? I didn't understand why you were letting him do that to me, why you were letting him kiss—"

"Stop. Please. Stay over there, okay?" He held his hands out in front of him, like he was warning her away. "I'm hanging on by a thread here, baby."

Good. Then it was working.

"When we got home, Rye made me take a shower. He said you wouldn't like that his scent was all over me. He said it would make you angry." She fingered the hem of the shirt she was wearing. "I used your soap, and I put on your clothes. I thought it would help if the only shifter on me was you."

"Do you know what you're doing right now? What you're asking? If we do this, your life changes. You can't go to Nevada. You can't go to parties and get high. You can't...damnit, Axie, you'll never be free." He swallowed. Even the slight movement of his throat was sexy and aroused her. "If we do this, if I take you, then you're *mine*."

After everything they'd been through to get to this point, he was still trying to put distance between them. But she understood now, and saw it for what it was. He didn't want to cage her. He didn't want to force her into another life she didn't want. And she loved him all the more for it. It had never been about him not wanting her, not caring about her. From the moment they met he'd put her safety, her happiness above his own.

"I want to be yours." She grabbed the hem of the shirt she was wearing, pulling it off and letting it fall to the ground. "I want to be here to make you laugh, to push your buttons. I want to watch you make me coffee every morning, and fall asleep as you put these dumb marks all over my body."

"You'll live here with me? You'll stay in Haxton?" He took a small step, hesitant and wide-eyed. "You won't resent me? You won't long to run away?"

"I'm not going anywhere. I don't want to go anywhere that you aren't." She hooked her thumbs in her shorts, pushing them down her legs, standing before him in only her panties. "Jace, you *are* my freedom."

She saw the exact moment he snapped, the moment his shifter took control. His eyes went so dark they appeared black. He leapt over the couch, landing in front of her and then standing to his full height. Her heart was pounding, the heat in her veins spreading through her whole body, ready to consume them both.

"You're *mine*."

She pulled her bottom lip through her teeth, smiling as he tackled her to the floor.

Chapter Thirty-Seven
Jace

Jace lifted Axie off her feet, moving with supernatural speed to lay her on the rug in front of the fireplace. The flames danced on her skin, creating beautiful shadows that he could have spent hours watching. But Jace wasn't in control right now. He'd handed it over to his wolf, to his instinct.

He hovered over her, kissing her lips, her jaw. His hands roamed the length of her body, cupping her breasts, pinching her perfect pink nipples. His dick was harder than it'd ever been in his life, and his heart was beating wildly in his chest. This, what was happening, the girl lying under him, these were things that he never thought he'd have. Things he never thought he'd want.

But, fuck, did he want her.

Axie pulled his shirt over his head, flinging it behind her onto the ground. Her fingers moved between them, unbuttoning his pants and then pushing them down as far as she could reach. He helped the rest of the way, kicking them off. Axie's panties were the only thing separating them.

He settled between her silky thighs, his dick jerking at her nearness. "Tell me again, baby."

Axie reached up, her fingertips tracing his face like she wanted to commit every feature to memory. "You're my freedom, Jace."

"And this wolf that's about to claim you?" His words were shaky. He was truly nervous to hear her answer, although it wouldn't change anything, because there was no going back, not now.

"Well, he's the best part." She smiled playfully, like she was about to share a secret. "Because that wolf, he's my wild."

Wild and free.

Jace and his wolf…together, they could give her everything.

He grabbed her panties, easily snapping the thin sides, letting them fall. He lined the head of his cock up with her entrance, pushing into her wet core slowly. He watched her face, saw how good he was making her feel, her pleasure increasing with every inch of himself he gave her. Nothing had ever felt as good as her pussy wrapped around him. It was more than he could have ever imagined it would be.

He wanted to live inside her body.

Jace stilled, breathing in her scent mixing with his, appreciating the moment he buried himself as far as he could go. Axie's nails dug into the flesh of his ass, urging him to move: to make her come, to make her truly his.

He pulled out, then surged back in, dropping his head to his chest. "Baby."

"Jace." She hiked her leg farther up his hip, tilting her head back with her eyes closed. "Don't stop."

He braced his hands on either side of her, his thrusts increasing in strength and speed. He felt his release already start to build, chills racing across his fevered flesh. Axie's skin was heated against his, her body crying out for the bond, demanding it. He nipped at her breasts as they bounced each time he hammered into her. He had to put his hand on her shoulder to hold her in place, his wolf losing all sense of control.

He growled as he dipped down to lick up the column of her slender throat, whispering against the shell of her ear. "Open your eyes, baby." He bit her jaw, demanding she do as he said. He rose up above her, meeting her dark gaze with his own.

"Jace, yes, so fucking close." She wet her lips as his hand moved to her neck, squeezing lightly to keep her where he wanted her. "More."

His shifter responded, increasing his pressure, loving everything about the way she wanted to be claimed. He slowed, dragging his dick out of her perfect pussy, prolonging the moment between them. She whimpered at the loss of his fullness, her eyes pleading with him, begging.

"*Mine.*" He tightened his hold even more, sinking his hips deep, surging back in her. He buried himself to the hilt, rocking in place, making her gasp. "You belong to me, *say it.*" He was so close, he could feel his orgasm coming like a tidal wave.

"Yes, fuck, yes I belong to you." She whimpered, her nails scraping down his back, making him shiver in pleasure. "You and your wolf."

His wolf roared in appreciation, and he pulled out one more time before slamming back inside her as far as he could possibly go. Her pussy milked his dick, like a tight relentless fist, her orgasm dragging his from his body. He kept his eyes on hers as he spilled inside her, pulsing so fucking hard that it almost hurt.

Hurt so good.

They were bonded together now forever. Axie was his mate, and he was hers. It was almost strange that such a big thing was over in a matter of seconds. There was no ceremony, no words spoken. But the commitment was there, he could feel the warmth of it settle on his soul.

Jace refused to leave her body, even after the shock waves of both their orgasms started to die down. She'd have to kick him out if she ever wanted to get off the floor. Her eyes were closed now, her chest still heaving. He moved his hand from her throat, wincing at the red marks he'd left behind. Was he too rough?

"Are you okay?" His voice sounded scratchy to his own ears. "Axie?"

"Hmm?" She grinned, nodding with what he hoped was blissful sigh.

"Did I hurt you? I've never, um, done that before."

She opened one eye. "Claimed a mate? Well, I should fucking hope not." She pursed her lips, drawing Jace's attention to the fact they were red and swollen from his kisses. "*I* don't share."

His own lips twitched at her joke, although the last thing he wanted to be thinking about right now was what Jasper and Riley got up to in bed. "I've never had sex before."

Both eyes popped open and her brows rose to wrinkle her forehead. "You're a virgin?"

He glanced down between them, where her pussy was still full of him. "I *was*."

"How is that possible? You went down on me like a fucking pro."

He couldn't help but snort with laughter, because only Axie would talk so openly like that. Maybe Riley was right. She and his twin did have a lot in common. "Thanks for the compliment, baby."

He licked her bottom lip, taking it between his teeth and tugging. "I said I'd never had sex, but I wasn't like a saint or anything."

"If you never wanted a mate, never thought you'd have one, then what were you waiting for?"

It was a valid question, and one she deserved the answer to, no matter how painful it was for him to talk about. Would it make her hate him? Was it possible now for her to feel that emotion when it came to him? She belonged to him, forever.

"My father thought women were a weakness, beneath him, a means to an end."

She nodded. "I know. I met him a few times growing up. I was too mouthy around him, pissing him off on purpose, so my father started locking me away when he came to the house."

Jace grinned at the image, Axie as a child, dark hair down to her waist as she glared up at his imposing father.

"He would bring girls to the house, women, as casually as he was bringing home takeout for dinner. He'd send them to my room, expecting me to have sex with them, to use them the way he did." Sometimes the girls were young, closer to Jace's age. And sometimes they looked old enough to be his mother. They never seemed scared, like they were being forced against their will. But every time one of them would push his bedroom door open, he'd feel sick to his stomach. "It was another way for him to control me, to groom me to be exactly like him." Axie stayed quiet, lying under him, trailing her fingertips along his bare back. "I knew he'd be mad if I sent them away untouched, but I refused to have sex with them. It was like this private stand I took for myself."

Axie moved one hand to his hair, tugging lightly. "Well, you're really good at it." She pushed at his shoulders, rolling him onto his back. "Was it everything you thought it would be?"

The sight of her on top of him, the fire lighting her beautiful face, was making his cock start to harden inside her all over again. "It was better than I could have ever imagined." He cupped her breasts, rolling her nipples between his fingers. "Did I hurt you?" His eyes moved to her neck.

"No." She scraped her nails down his chest, making him hiss. "I like it when you lose control."

"Yeah?" Jace sat up, keeping her tight against him. "That's good, because I feel close to losing it again." He threaded one hand in her wild hair, the other went to her lower back. "That okay with you?"

She closed her eyes, moaning as she rested her forehead against his, nodding.

He kissed her mouth as she started rocking her body, her pussy flooding them both with pleasure. He didn't know if he'd ever get enough of this, enough of Axie.

His mate.

Jace took her hips in his hands, gripping them tightly, demanding she give him more. She shoved him down on his back, grinding on top of him. She moved his grip from her hip to her breasts, showing him how she wanted him to touch her. His girl liked to ride that fine line between pleasure and pain. And it was her trust in him that turned him on the most. He was stronger than her, driven by instinct and desire. But she knew he'd never hurt her, and she was right.

He watched the way she let her head fall back, her long hair swaying behind her. His marks were peppered all over her flesh, the sight of them making his shifter want to howl. She belonged to them, in every way. He clenched his teeth, the need to possess her crawling up his spine, taking hold of his heart. He'd already claimed her, but he wanted to do it again and again until his release was spilling down her thighs.

He roared, grabbing her by the throat and pushing her onto her back. He nipped at her jaw, licking to take the sting away. He thrust into her, making her small body jerk each time. And she smiled at him, because she fucking loved it.

"Baby," he growled against her neck, his balls tightening in anticipation. "I want to hear you scream for me." He buried himself inside her, grinding against her clit as he bit down harshly on her shoulder. "Fuck, baby."

"Don't stop." She urged him to give her more, her hands on his ass. "Please don't stop."

He stayed deep in her pussy, refusing to lose even an inch, keeping his hips flush against hers. They were both covered in sweat, the sounds of their pleasure filling the large room. He never wanted it to end, the line he was riding, the fine edge right before he knew his orgasm would hit. He wanted her core to tighten. He wanted her body to drag his release from his. "Come for me, baby, I want to *feel* you come."

Axie gasped when he bit her again, the pain triggering her pussy, causing it to clench, fisting him in that fucking epic way he'd already become addicted to. She screamed his name, her nails drawing blood from his flesh. He let go, spilling inside her, flooding her body until he had nothing left to give.

Their chests were heaving as they tried to catch their breath. But this time, he pulled out of her, sitting back on his knees.

"What are you doing?" Her words came out in short pants, her hands pushing her wild hair off her flushed face.

Jace stared at her pussy, watching as his seed leaked from her body. He could hear her questioning him, but he couldn't find the words to answer. His shifter loved what he saw. He wanted her to be full of him, always. Jace reached a finger out, gathering his come, putting it back inside her where it belonged.

"I'm guessing the wolf is feeling a bit self-satisfied right now?" She used her foot to push gently at his chest. "Such a primal little wolf, isn't he?"

Jace tore his eyes away from her core, meeting her smiling gaze. "Little?" He shook his head, climbing to his feet. "He certainly doesn't like being called little." He stared down at her beautiful naked body, her hair spread out all around her. "And he doesn't want you to stand up." He pursed his lips, glancing back to her pussy. "Gravity isn't his friend."

Axie laughed, the sound making him smile. "Young, dumb, and full of come. Who knew that song was actually about shifters?"

He snorted, loving the odd things that tended to come out of her pouty lips.

Chapter Thirty-Eight
Axie

Axie and Jace were in his bed, lying naked and pressed close together. He'd carried her from the living room, taking her into his bedroom instead of upstairs to the one she'd been using since she got here. He'd drawn her a hot bath, climbing in behind her, washing her until she was clean and relaxed.

His room was exactly what she'd thought it'd be. Black paint covered his walls, black curtains on his windows. There was a navy suede loveseat against one wall, and a massive TV took up another. And his bed? A huge four-poster made of fired steel that made it appear blue. The only brightness in the room were his stark white blankets, like the ones in her room upstairs.

They were both resting on their sides, his front to her back. He was marking her with his scent, with his teeth. "That was a dangerous game you played earlier, taunting my wolf like that."

"I was ready, you were ready." Axie rolled over to face him. "I needed to make sure you didn't have a chance to think too hard about what was happening." Her tapped her finger against his forehead. "Jace uses this too much." She kissed his chest, right over his heart. "I needed you to use this instead." She smirked, reaching down to palm his dick. "And this."

He moved in her hand, semi-hard already. "It won't go down." He frowned, almost pouting. "My wolf likes being inside his mate."

She stroked him lazily. "And you?"

"I like making love with my girl."

Axie was pretty sure she swooned for the first time in her life. "I guess you're not so different after all, you and your shifter." She'd never be able to think of them like he did, like they were separate, battling it out for control.

"The more I give in to what he wants, the better we seem to get along." He pulled her closer. "When we were in the van, watching you and Riley, and Baze commanded me to stand down, my shifter listened. He knew his alpha was in charge and he instantly complied. It was me, my human side that couldn't seem to get on board. I knew you wouldn't like Riley's hands on you." His lips touched her forehead softly. "I was too close to you, your body would revolt at Riley touching you like that, and I hated that you were going to feel uncomfortable."

Axie stayed quiet, wanting him to keep going, to keep sharing. Every time he opened up to her, let her in, she could almost see the last few frayed edges of his soul knitting back together. They were healing each other, from the inside out.

"My shifter wants to own you, he wants to take care of you and worship you. He wants you to wear his mark, his scent. Protect you." He paused, his hand cupping her cheek. "I want to love you, baby."

A tear fell down her cheek, the smallest happiest tear she'd ever cried.

***

"Okay, yeah, we'll see you when you get back." Axie opened her eyes, loving waking up to the sound of Jace's voice. "I'll call a meeting, but there are a few things I need to figure out first." He was speaking quietly, like he didn't want to wake her. "Drive safe." He hung up, setting his cell back on the nightstand, and then he lay down beside her.

"Everything okay?" She pulled the blankets up under her chin and snuggled into his arms.

"Baze, Pen, and Jasper are headed back to the house." He kissed the top of her no doubt messy hair. "They're bringing breakfast. You hungry?"

She nodded, hiking her leg over his hip. "Someone depleted all my energy last night."

"Someone needs to move their pussy away from someone's dick, or someone's going to be forced to deplete some more." Jace tickled her ribs, making her squirm and giggle.

"Man, who knew all this time the only thing you needed in order to be in a good mood was sex?" She climbed on top of him, straddling his lap, his hard length inches from her core. "Your pack better thank me." She took his hands off her breasts, pinning them to the mattress by his head. "Maybe they'll pay me a monthly stipend for my services? My father cut me off. I'm broke as a joke."

"You're not broke." He took one of his hands back, fisting his dick, stroking it a few times as he smirked up at her. "What's mine is yours, and what's mine? Is plentiful."

"Silly shifter." She shook her head, letting her long hair hang around them like a curtain. "You think because you claimed me I'm going to spend the rest of my life barefoot and pregnant in your kitchen?"

"First of all, no one cooks in *our* kitchen but me." Her grabbed her hips, positioning her over his cock, pulling her down on him at the same time he thrust up, both gasping at they met in the middle. "Second of all, I'm not ready for babies, but my wolf has other ideas, so you better be on some good birth control."

Axie used her knees and her core, riding him expertly, loving the way his dark eyes rolled back in his head. She didn't need to answer him, because she knew he didn't really care. If she lied and told him she wasn't on birth control, he wouldn't do things any differently. His instinct wouldn't allow it. He'd come inside her, filling her up every fucking chance he got.

"Harder," he commanded, urging her to stop toying with him.

She refused, keeping the same lazy pace.

"Axie, fuck me, or I'm going to take back control."

"For someone who only started having sex twelve hours ago, you sure are bossy."

He growled, the sound a low warning as he popped her ass.

Axie swooped down, biting the space where his shoulder met his neck, sucking on his skin until she was sure he'd wear her mark too. Then she sat up, grinding her hips on top of him while he was deep inside her. She leaned back, changing the angle, making him hiss. His hands flew to her waist, moving her body at the speed he wanted her to fuck him. He was close, and he was losing control. She watched, unable to tear her eyes away. His abs tightened, his forearms flexed.

"Baby, fuck, you feel so good."

His words turned her on, she felt his rough tone down to her bones and both pushed her closer to falling. "Keep talking, please, your voice…" When he spoke like that, her body responded.

"You like that, Axie?" His eyes opened, taking in her naked body as she moved on top of him, nodding. "You want me to tell you how good you feel? How perfect your pussy feels?" She nodded again, their eyes locking. "Because it does, it feels so fucking good, baby." His hand slid up her front, his palm covering her slender throat. "But you want to know what my favorite part is?" She whimpered in reply. "My favorite part is when you come for me, when that perfect pussy starts to milk my dick." He used his hold to pull her closer, the added pressure to her clit making her cry out his name. "Can you do that for me, baby?" She nodded, her hips moving faster, chasing her release. "Come for me, Axie."

His words were a command and her body instantly complied, her orgasm hitting her hard, taking her breath away.

Her name was on his lips, the veins in his neck bulging as he came, filling her up all over again.

Chapter Thirty-Nine
Jace

Jace had every intention that he and Axie would be dressed and casually sitting in the kitchen by the time his family got home. But thanks to his new and unquenchable sex drive, they walked into a room already filled with people. There were bakery boxes on the island, a fresh pot of coffee sitting on a cork hot pad.

He was holding her hand, and he had a massive bite mark on his neck. She'd covered some of his marks with makeup, which irritated his shifter to no end. They were both in jeans. Jace rarely wore jeans, preferring slacks because that was what he was used to. But Axie had found them in his closet and demanded he wear them.

He'd do anything she asked him to.

"Morning." Riley glanced at Axie, then him. "Ax forgave me last night, for what happened, but, um, I wanted to tell you I was sorry." His winced, his eyes pleading for mercy. Riley didn't like conflict, it made him feel unsettled, which was why he was always trying to stop Jasper from pissing Jace off.

"He forgives you." Axie backhanded Jace in the chest. "Right, Jace?"

He sighed as he held his hand out for Riley to shake. "You didn't do anything wrong. There's nothing to forgive."

Jasper choked on the sip of coffee he'd taken. "*Nothing to forgive?* I didn't know sex could be so good that it changed someone's personality."

"That's because you've never had sex with *me*," Axie spoke coolly as she reached forward and plucked a pastry out of the nearest box.

Jasper laughed loud, high-fiving her across the island. "Nice."

Baze met Jace's eyes, like he was wary of how he'd respond to their teasing banter. Jace shrugged, kissing the top of his girl's head as he poured her a cup of coffee. Pen reached up from her spot beside him, rubbing his back like she was proud of him.

Two days ago, he'd have punched his twin for that comment, no doubt. So maybe Jasper was right, maybe Axie had changed him. "I need to go torture a bad guy." At least a little. Jace patted his mate's ass, feeling okay about leaving her here with his family while he went to "accidentally" kill the man who had hurt her. Now that Axie was truly his, her body would stop demanding the bond, and his twin wouldn't be a threat.

"No need, bro." Jasper spoke around a mouth full of banana nut muffin. "I had violence before breakfast."

Jace's eyes widened in surprise. "You did?"

"Yep. And I got a name." Jasper pulled a piece of paper from his shorts pocket, sliding it across the island toward him. "You recognize that guy from your research?"

Jace picked it up, reading Jasper's chicken scratch. "Unfortunately."

The guy who'd gone after Axie was a drug runner for the cartel, a sort of glorified middleman who had been steadily rising in the ranks over the last couple of years. Jace had only met him once even though Franklin worked him with often.

Riley sat down next to Jasper, stealing the rest of his muffin. "What'd you do with the prisoner?"

Jace had grown up talking about death and destruction over pancakes: this was all normal to him. But when had it become commonplace for his twin and his best friend? Had he done this to them?

"Baze and I took care of it." Jasper pointed to their alpha. "Let's leave it at, he joined some other bad guys, somewhere that they'll never be found."

Once again, his twin had killed for him. Jasper had murdered the man who hurt his mate, and although Jace would have really enjoyed doing it himself, he was impressed at Jasper's initiative. Which kind of spoke to the point that Jace had caused all this, had taught them that this was normal everyday life.

That wasn't what Jace wanted for his family, for his pack. He wanted the danger to go away, not to have death become so ingrained in who they were that burying a man in the backyard was something they did before their coffee.

"What now? We go after this dickwad?" Jasper tapped the slip of paper Jace had refolded.

Go after him and do what? Hand him more power? Kill him because he thought to touch Jace's girl? What would happen after that? Take out another bad guy and someone else tries to rise up. It was a never-ending cycle. It was in that moment that Jace realized things needed to change. And that it was up to him to make it happen.

"No. Call a pack meeting, I need to talk to everyone." He waited until Baze took out his phone, doing what he'd demanded, not asked. "But first, I need to talk to my girl." He reached for Axie's hand, pulling her out of the kitchen toward his office as she finished her pastry.

He closed the door as she hopped on his desk, licking her fingers clean. "You really want to talk to me, or is your dick hard?" She grinned, her gaze darting to his crotch.

There it was again, a moment where his mate reminded him of his twin. It was a little bit fucked up. The universe hadn't made a mistake, but it sure as hell had a sick sense of humor.

He turned his computer monitor around so she could see the numerous files he had open. "My father had dossiers on every single man he encountered. He traded in blackmail and secrets, calling in favors for people when it would benefit him the most."

"Ah, like Lucifer." She nodded, sagely.

Lucifer? Good lord. "Stop hanging out with Riley, television rots your brain." He pointed to the screen. "I've been reading these files, taking in every bad deed these men have ever done. Drugs, guns, sex trafficking. These are the worst kind of people. I know the man who will most likely take over now that Franklin is gone, I've met him, and he's soulless. He's worse than my father in so many ways. And the thought of calling a meeting with him and handing him the supremacy he's after… I don't know if I can do it. I don't know if I can have a part in making a man like that even more powerful."

"What do you want to do?"

"I want to destroy them all, one by one."

It had clicked in the kitchen while he was listening to the way Jasper had spent his morning. Jace was raised in the middle of bullshit like this, and his pack had been dragged into it. When they'd killed Franklin, he and Jasper had laid their monster to rest, but not *all* the monsters who worked with their evil father.

Condoning another one of those fuckers to take their father's place wouldn't solve their problems; it would only create new ones.

"And I want to use *your* father to do it."

Chapter Forty
Jace

He'd stood in front of his mate and asked her if he could use her father as a scapegoat, effectively asking her to sign his death certificate with her own hand. And she hadn't hesitated to say yes. Axie had been right when she'd stood toe-to-toe with him in the guest bedroom. She and Jace were more alike than they were different.

They'd been raised by heartless men who had intentionally deprived them of love and affection. They'd wanted to get out, to be free. And now, they would be. Axie wasn't a weakness: she was pure strength. She'd endured, she'd survived, and she was perfect for him.

Jace stood in front of the fireplace, his lips twitching as he took a moment to remember the things he and Axie had done here last night. He glanced across the room, meeting her gaze. She winked, biting her lip the way his shifter couldn't seem to handle. He needed to get the pack meeting over with so he could take his mate back to his bed.

"I know that I told you I wanted to meet with the man most likely to take over now that Franklin was gone. I wanted to give him my blessing, I wanted him to go about his business and leave us alone. But I was wrong to think that was the right choice." He watched as Riley stood behind Axie, rocking Hadley while holding her bottle. "Nothing matters more to me than this pack's safety. And maybe this guy would leave us alone, but what about the next one? Would he come after our kids?" Jasper had his hand resting on Maddi's stomach and Linc kept shoving it off. "Could I sleep at night knowing that I did nothing to stop the cycle?" He shook his head. "I don't think I could." No one spoke when he paused. "Axie and I talked with Mathias about an hour ago and came up with a new plan."

Jasper pouted, crossing his arms over his chest. "So now *she's* on your team and I'm out?"

Axie leaned forward, peering around Pen, grinning. "That's what life-changing sex will get you."

"Will you two stop?" Riley placed a now-sleeping Hadley in Jasper's arms. "Here, practice being still and quiet enough to keep a sleeping baby from waking up."

"Do we have to involve Mathias in everything we do now?" Linc rolled his eyes.

"Wait, you two had sex?" Maddi's jaw dropped open. "Does that mean what I think it means?"

"Yeah, it means Jace isn't a virgin anymore," Jasper spoke softly and in a high-pitched voice, like that would help keep Hadley snoozing.

"Not even a little bit," Axie added, bumping the fist his twin held out.

"You were a virgin?" Dom's eyebrows rose in surprise. "I didn't see that coming."

"You often think about eighteen-year-old boys' sex lives, babe?" Corey cocked her head to the side.

"We're going to leak the dirt we have on every single guy my father ever worked with." Jace talked over his pack, glad that his statement seemed to get everyone's attention, making all eyes snap back to the front of the room. "We can't hand it over to the feds, because these men lawyer up pretty fucking quick, we all know that. We've seen it happen." Jace held his hand out, loving that Axie instantly stood and came to his side.

"But what would happen if there were no attorneys to turn to? Jace wanted to have it look like the information was leaked from my father's office, making him a target and keeping our hands cleans. But." Axie held up a finger, adding a dramatic pause as she enjoyed this part of their plan the most because it was her idea. "Why stop there? My father is one of many lawyers in Colorado who help these evil men get out of jail time and time again. I made a list, and Mathias did some digging. Every lawyer will leak information on their specific clients, giving these guys no one they know to help them. Sure, they can pay to bring in other lawyers, but how do they refute the information their old attorneys have on them?"

"That's brilliant." Riley's eyes lit up. "It's perfect."

"It's still dangerous." Jace put his hands on Axie's shoulders, pulling her back against him. "Mathias is good at what he does, and he assured me that none of this could be traced back to us. But we're still going to be in the vicinity of a kicked hornet's nest."

"We're going to do this slowly, a little bit at a time, over the next six months." Axie was smart, and whether she wanted to admit it or not, she'd picked up a lot of knowledge from her father over the years. "We don't want to send everyone into a full-blown panic, we don't want anyone going into hiding. We're going to be systematic. Careful." Jace laughed to himself, because those were two things Axie was not. And listening to her explain their plan to the pack was making him want to carry her to bed and demand she turn back into his wild mate.

"Okay, what do you need from us, bubs?" Pen. Always asking him how she could help, always so kind.

"Stay safe, don't take risks, and stay aware of your surroundings." Jace couldn't lock everyone away. He couldn't demand they stop living their lives. He couldn't make them prisoners. He knew because he'd suggested it, and Axie had shot it down instantly. "If I ask you to stay home, don't argue with me, know I'm doing it because something is about to go down. If I need you to spend the weekend here in the mountains, don't fight me."

"We can do that." Molly looked at her mate. "Right?"

Keller nodded, a soft look on his face. "Right."

Jace didn't know how long it would take for them to rid this part of the country of as much evil as they could. He wasn't naïve. He knew that bad people were born, or created, every day. He was one man. He couldn't save the world. But he could keep the people he loved safe. And he could try to ensure that their next generation would never know the type of violence he'd witnessed growing up.

And that was enough.

He wrapped his arms around Axie, squeezing her tight as he put his mouth next to her ear. "I love you, baby." She turned in his embrace, smiling up at him like he hung the moon.

"Are we going to talk about the fact that our beta is mated up?" Jace looked over Axie's head at Linc. "He clearly told that smoke show he loved her, we all heard it."

"Did you just call her a smoke show?" Molly backhanded him. "*Your* mate is right next to you."

Maddi waved away her friend's concern. "His mate agrees. Axie is fucking gorgeous." She fanned her face. "It must be the hormones, because watching the two of them fight the urge to tear each other's clothes off is making me hot as hell."

"If we're bringing shit up, are we going to talk about the fact that Pen is pregnant?" Keller raised his hand. "I mean, we can all hear the baby's heartbeat by now, right?"

"I can't." Corey pointed at Pen's chest. "But her boobs have doubled in size."

"I'm pregnant. Surprise." Pen sent Keller a withering glare. "I wanted to wait until my first doctor's appointment so I could hear the heartbeat too." Pen stood, tearing up as she returned everyone's hugs. "Bubs ordered me a Doppler so I can listen to it whenever I want to now."

Every female in the room said awww in unison.

"So, Pen's pregnant, Axie is here to stay, and Jace has surprisingly overturned Riley's reign as the sweetest, most thoughtful male in this pack. Does that about sum it up?" Linc clapped his hands together once. "Okay, good, can we eat lunch now?"

"I'm starving." Maddi rubbed her stomach, leaning her head against Jasper's arm. "Me and this little girl need our guys to feed us."

"We grabbed Chinese food on the way." Corey spoke up above everyone, taking Hadley from Jasper. "It's in the kitchen."

Jace kept Axie pressed against his front as the two of them watched their pack file out of the room to go make a mess of the kitchen. He kissed her neck. "You hungry, baby?"

She turned again and hopped up into his arms, wrapping her legs around his waist. "Yes." She kissed his eager lips, tangling her tongue with his, swallowing his deep moan. "Now ask me *what* I'm hungry for."

"I got you, baby." He sucked playfully at her neck as he carried her through the living room and into the crowded kitchen. "Grab some food." He paused long enough for her to pluck two white containers off the island, then carted her out of the room, the sound of the pack's commentary following after them.

"They better not have gotten the box with my egg rolls."

"Leave them alone, there's enough egg rolls to go around."

"Riley, do you kiss everyone's ass? Or do you and Axie have that weird bond like you have with Corey?"

"Maybe Axie is pregnant and Riley is destined to be obsessed with that baby too."

"Already? Is that even possible?"

"Dom knocked me up on night one."

"I'm just that good."

"From what I heard last night, Jace may be that good too."

"Did Riley just make a sex joke?"

"You guys think Riley is so innocent, but let me tell you, the things I've watched that guy do…"

Jace slammed their bedroom door shut, tossing a laughing Axie on the bed. He crawled up her body, putting their food on the nightstand for later.

Much, much later.

Epilogue
Jace

Three Months Later

Jace made coffee, a large pot. He'd had to order a new machine since more people than his mate and him lived in his house. Baze and Pen had started to build their home a few acres away from his on the land he'd gifted them. Pen wanted to be settled and in full nesting mode by the time the baby was born. Jace had a contact in a construction company that employed mainly shifters. They were stronger than human males, they had more endurance, could see at night, and overall, worked faster. The new home should be completed in six months.

He'd enjoyed every minute of living with his alpha and Pen, but now that Axie was truly his, he didn't need them like he used to. There wasn't a constant threat of loneliness coursing through his heart anymore. And his peaceful moments were plentiful.

"Is the coffee ready? Can you make omelets too?" Jasper came into the kitchen, stealing the early morning silence. "I'm fucking starving."

Jasper and Riley spent more nights here than they did in their own apartment in town. Jace found it comical, and annoying, especially since Jasper had complained like a child every time he'd had to stay in the mountains for his own safety.

"Aren't you supposed to be living two hours away from here by now?" Jace pulled out a carton of eggs from the refrigerator, then cheese, bell peppers, and onions. "Classes start in three days."

Both his twin and their best friend were supposed to have moved to Greenly weeks ago. But for some reason they kept putting it off. They had logical excuses every time Jace brought it up: their apartment wasn't ready, Maddi had a doctor appointment, or Hadley wasn't feeling well.

"Yeah." Jasper took a sip of his coffee, wincing like it was still too hot. "Um, about that."

"Oh, are you finally going to tell him?" Axie breezed into the room, piling her hair on the top of her head as she leaned in for a good morning kiss. She'd still been asleep when Jace had woken an hour ago.

Some mornings he chose to stay in bed, watching her sleep, content to simply lie beside her. But that morning he'd gone for a run, knowing that he wouldn't be able to the rest of the week.

"Going to tell me what?" Jace kept one hand on Axie's hip as he expertly cracked eggs into a skillet with the other.

"I'm not going to school." Jasper shrugged, as casually as if he was discussing his plans for the day.

Jace turned his back on the eggs on the stove, thankful when Axie took over breakfast. She'd convinced Jace to teach her to cook and she wasn't half bad. "What do you mean you're not going? Why the hell not?"

"You finally told him?" Riley came in, pouring himself a cup of coffee. "Took you long enough."

"Someone better start talking, now." Jace used his beta tone, making his statement a command.

Axie busied herself, tossing the chopped vegetables into the skillet. Riley took another sip of his coffee, trying to hide his face inside the mug.

"After everything that happened this summer, I decided it wasn't a good time to move so far away from everyone." Jasper met Jace's gaze, not backing down. "Things have gone well with the first few information leaks, but who's to say it'll always be that way? I told you we were in this together, and I meant it. I'm not leaving Haxton until all this shit is over."

"No." Jace shook his head. "I'm not going to let you put off school because of this. You want to play ball, you want that whole frat strap college experience. I'm fine here, I have the rest of the pack and—"

"And the rest of the pack is too busy with their growing families." Jasper cut him off. "Hadley, Maddi's little girl, Pen's kid. There are going to be babies popping out all over the damn place.

The coaches have jobs, mates: families. They can't help you, not like I can."

Jace had grown up alone, abused, and longing for a better life. But he'd never in a million years imagined that he'd actually *get it*. He had a girl who loved him, and a brother who was willing to stand by his side. Jasper was putting what he wanted on hold to help Jace. To help their pack.

"What about Riley? You guys are supposed to live together."

Jasper patted their friend on his back. "It's one semester. I think he can survive without me for a few months." He pursed his lips. "And it's Riley. He'll be home to visit every weekend Corey and Hadley anyway."

"So you're going to stay here, in Haxton, and help me?" Jace fought his instinct to argue, choosing instead to lean into this new life of his. The one where he didn't insist that he didn't need anyone, because that wasn't the truth, not anymore.

"I'm going to stay here, *in this house*, and help you." Jasper grinned, popping some cheese into his mouth.

"This house?" Jace frowned, turning to Axie when he heard her giggle. "You knew about all this?"

She nodded, trying and failing to fold the omelet. "I did. And it looks like your breakfast just became scrambled eggs."

"You, me, Baze, Pen, and Jasper." Jace wrinkled his forehead, counting people on his fingers. "We're all going to live here together."

"Jasper talked to me about it a few weeks ago. He wanted to make sure that it was okay with me." Axie twisted off the burner then wrapped her arms around his waist. "And it is."

Of course it was. Axie and Jasper were two peas in a damn pod.

"No one thought to make sure *I* was okay with it?" Jace knew he was fighting a losing battle, but his personality demanded he at least try.

His mate moved her arms to his neck, hoisting herself up and wrapping her legs around his waist. He automatically palmed her ass, his dick stirring at her nearness. "We knew you would be, although you'd pretend to hate it. And if you were too obstinate, we had a plan B."

"What was plan B?"

Axie moved her mouth to his ear. "I was going to fuck you until you were too tired to protest anymore."

Jace's hands tightened on her ass, a low growl coming from his chest.

"It's a good plan B, huh?" Jasper winked, grabbing the skillet and filling plates for him and Riley.

"Is plan B what I think it is?" Riley spoke around a mouthful of eggs.

"Yep." Jasper gestured with his head toward the living room. "Come on, Rye, let's go eat as far away from their bedroom as possible. Listening to them fuck makes me horny and we've got to move me into this mansion today."

"You're moving in today? Like all your shit? Into my house?" Jace was glaring across the kitchen, watching his brother and best friend retreat while his mate placed kisses along his throat.

"It's *our* house now, bro." Jasper's laughter floated in from the living room.

"It's not his house." Jace sat Axie on the kitchen island, pouting. "He's not living here forever, right?"

"No, of course not." Axie slipped her hand down his pants, stroking his rigid cock. "If he's still here two years from now, we can build him a house next to Baze and Pen."

"We?" Jace liked the sound of that considering Axie had a hard time accepting money from him.

"What's yours is mine and what's yours…" She licked the shell of his ear as she stroked his dick. "Is plentiful."

Jace dropped his head to her shoulder, his control slipping with each twist of her hand. "Maybe one day when we live alone, we can fuck on the kitchen counter." He sucked at the flesh on her slender throat.

"Why wait?" Axie's fingers moved to the button of his jeans, pulling out his hard length.

Jace gripped her hips, dragging her body closer to him. She brought out his wolf, demanding he love her in the wild way she knew he was capable of.

He tore through her leggings, exposing her wet pussy to his hungry gaze. He longed to taste her, to lay her out on the island and worship every inch of her body. But they lived in a house full of people. A damn shame there wasn't time for that. And it didn't look like there would be any *month* soon.

Jace lined up to her core, sinking inside her warm heat, groaning at how fucking good she felt wrapped around him. "Baby."

"Jace." Axie spoke his name in a breathless whimper.

It was always like this between them, always mind-blowing. He wasn't sure he'd ever get his fill of her.

One of his hands was on her hip, the other on her shoulder, holding her in place as he drove into her over and over. He fused his lips to hers, trying like hell to stifle the moans starting to tear out of her throat. "You've got to be quiet, baby." Someone could walk in any second and that reality had them chasing down their orgasms as quickly as possible. He fisted his hand in her hair, tugging against her scalp, making her whimper. "Shhhh."

"Well stop doing things that make me want to scream your damn name."

He moved both palms to her ass, holding her in place as he hammered into her. "You close, Axie?"

She nodded, her lip between her teeth, trying hard to stay silent.

Jace loved the look in her green eyes, like she was begging him to help her. He cradled her head, moving her mouth to his shoulder. "Come for me, baby." She bit down hard, her moans muffled by his flesh, her pussy milking his dick exactly the way he liked it: relentless and hard, dragging his orgasm from his body. He spilled inside her, wave after wave consuming them both.

They stayed like that, connected and panting for breath for a few more blissful moments before Axie lifted her head.

"You think they heard us?" Axie waggled her eyebrows, completely unfazed by the notion.

"They did," Jasper called from somewhere farther away than the living room. "And they're as impressed as they are disgusted. We eat on that counter."

Her gaze shot to Jace's, her expression almost guarded, as if she was wary of his reaction.

"We'll get a housekeeper, go the fuck away." Jace slipped out of his mate, pulled up his jeans, and then tossed her over his shoulder. "I think I need more of this plan B you came up with."

He slapped her ass, his brother's laughter following them all the way to their bedroom.

PLAYLIST

You Don't Own Me by Grace
New Americana by Halsey
Guys My Age by Hey Violet
Sucker for Pain by Lil' Wayne and Imagine Dragons
Tear In My Heart by Twenty One Pilots
I Don't Want to Live Forever by Zayn and Taylor Swift
You Should See Me In A Crown by Billie Eilish
Unholy by Hey Violet

ABOUT THE AUTHOR

L.P. lives in Austin, Texas with her husband, daughter, three rescue dogs, and one adopted cat. The first group of chickens met with a sad and unexpected death. They have been replaced. The dwarf goats are a story for another day. And now there are ducks.

Writer, business owner and office manager, L.P. says she loves to read as much as she loves to write. Reading a good book is her reward after writing one. In her spare time—ha!—she fosters puppies for a rescue organization based in Austin.

Connect with L.P. –

lpmaxa.wordpress.com

facebook.com/pages/LP-Maxa/1442560722667127

twitter.com/lpmaxa

instagram.com/lpmaxa

www.BOROUGHSPUBLISHINGGROUP.com

If you enjoyed this book, please write a review. Our authors appreciate the feedback, and it helps future readers find books they love. We welcome your comments and invite you to send them to info@boroughspublishinggroup.com. Follow us on Facebook, Twitter and Instagram, and be sure to sign up for our newsletter for surprises and new releases from your favorite authors.

Are you an aspiring writer? Check out www.boroughspublishinggroup.com/submit and see if we can help you make your dreams come true.